All Your Nights

Book Four, MacLarens of Fire Mountain Contemporary Western Romance

SHIRLEEN DAVIES

MACLARENS *of*
FIRE MOUNTAIN
━ CONTEMPORARY ━

Books Series by Shirleen Davies

Historical Western Romances

Redemption Mountain
MacLarens of Fire Mountain Historical
MacLarens of Boundary Mountain

Romantic Suspense

Eternal Brethren Military Romantic Suspense
Peregrine Bay Romantic Suspense

Contemporary Western Romance

MacLarens of Fire Mountain Contemporary
Macklins of Whiskey Bend

The best way to stay in touch is to subscribe to my newsletter. Go to my Website *www.shirleendavies.com* and fill in your email and name in the Join My Newsletter boxes. That's it!

Avalanche Ranch Press, LLC
PO Box 12618
Prescott, AZ 86304

Cover design by Sweet 'n Spicy Designs

Book design and conversions by Joseph Murray at 3rdplanetpublishing.com

ISBN: 978-1-941786-10-9

I care about quality, so if you find something in error, please contact me via email at **shirleen@shirleendavies.com**

Description

He lives on the edge. She's strictly by the book.

Kade Taylor likes living on the edge. As an undercover agent for the DEA and a former Special Ops team member, his current assignment seems tame—keep tabs on a bookish Ph.D. candidate the agency believes is connected to a ruthless drug cartel.

Brooke Sinclair is weeks away from obtaining her goal of a doctoral degree. She spends time finalizing her presentation and relaxing with another student who seems to want nothing more than her friendship. That's fine with Brooke. Her last serious relationship ended in a broken engagement.

Her future is set, safe and peaceful, just as she's always planned—until Agent Taylor informs her she's under suspicion for illegal drug activities.

Kade and his DEA team obtain evidence which exonerates Brooke while placing her in danger from those who sought to use her. As Kade races to take down the drug cartel while protecting Brooke, he must also find common ground with the former suspect—a woman he desires with increasing intensity.

At odds with her better judgment, Brooke finds the more time she spends with Kade, the more she's attracted to the complex, multi-faceted agent. But Kade holds secrets he knows Brooke will never understand or accept.

Can Kade keep Brooke safe while coming to terms with his past, or will he stay silent, ruining any future with the woman his heart can't let go?

All Your Nights, book four in the MacLarens of Fire Mountain Contemporary Western Romance series, is a standalone full-length novel with an HEA.

All Your Nights

Prologue

San Diego, California

"I guess I'd better get going." Brooke Sinclair checked her watch and slipped her handbag onto her shoulder. "Thanks so much for the movie and coffee. I had a great time."

"As always, it was my pleasure. Do you have time for dinner this weekend?" Paco Bujazan jumped from his seat to pull out her chair. "Perhaps Saturday?"

Brooke hadn't been dating. She didn't define her lunches, study sessions, casual dinners, and late night meetings for coffee with Paco as dates. In her mind, they were two friends sharing time together—quite a bit of time over the last several weeks. She'd returned from a visit to see her mother and stepfather in Fire Mountain, Arizona, determined to break free of the safe cocoon she'd built around herself after the painful breakup with her fiancé over a year before. Paco approached her a couple of days after her return, inviting her to lunch. She'd accepted and had seen him on a regular basis for weeks—as friends and nothing more.

"Saturday would be great."

"That's wonderful. I'll pick you up at seven." Paco seemed surprised and pleased she accepted.

They parted outside the café, Paco heading toward the house his family paid for overlooking the Pacific Ocean, and Brooke to her one bedroom apartment in a complex several blocks from campus. She looked around, feeling the damp, foggy air creeping over the bluffs. Considered a safe area, she nonetheless felt a strange sense of unease and searched for her car keys a block before the underground parking garage. She pulled her purse in front of her and rummaged inside, losing focus for a brief moment, slipping off a curb and stumbling into the busy street. She caught herself, turning her head a moment before being knocked to the ground. The image of a black rocket flashed through her mind a moment before she drifted into unconsciousness.

******

"What the hell happened?" Dennis Johnson, Kade's boss and DEA Special Agent in Charge, stormed toward Kade and glared at the undercover agent who stood toe to toe with him.

"She stepped right in front of me. I'd missed the light and had to circle around a different way. When I caught sight of her, she was no more than a block from her car. It happened so fast I couldn't swerve out of the way." Kade Taylor had been following Brooke for weeks, ever since she had begun spending an inordinate amount of time with Francisco "Paco" Bujazan, heir apparent to one of the largest drug cartels in Mexico.

"We need to speak with her. What did the doctors say?" Dennis let out a deep breath. He needed to speak with this witness now, not a few days from now.

"Concussion, scrapes, bruises. No broken bones but they want to keep her overnight." Kade paced a few feet to the end of the hall, looking out the window to the freeway below. She'd been out of emergency a couple of hours and transferred into her own room. In her wallet, Kade found a driver's license with California address, health insurance card, student identification, one credit card, and a few dollars. Nothing to tell anyone who should be called in case of emergency, for which Kade had been grateful. The agency wanted her for as long as possible.

"What did you tell them?"

"The truth. I showed them my badge and told them I'd contact her family. They know I'll be taking her with us as soon as she's released."

"Agent Taylor?"

The two agents broke eye contact and looked down the hall toward a short, spectacled man who emerged from Brooke's room.

"I'm Special Agent Taylor. This is Special Agent in Charge Johnson. How is she? What can you tell us?"

"I'm Doctor Ahmed. Miss Sinclair has suffered a severe concussion. I've ordered a CT scan and MRI to rule out any internal bleeding. If all checks out well, I expect she'll be released tomorrow." Dr. Ahmed removed his glasses before looking directly at Kade. "She does have someone to watch over her for a few days, correct?"

"Yes, sir, she does."

The doctor's face revealed his reservations as he gazed at the disheveled agent whose long hair had been secured with a leather cord at the back of his neck, his leathers sporting patches representative of his biker status.

"All right, just be certain she has someone nearby at all times. I want to see her immediately if anything worsens within the first seventy-two hours after her release." He shook both men's hands and turned toward the long hallway behind him.

Johnson's fisted hands settled on his waist. "I'll get someone to watch her tonight."

"No. I'm staying."

"You've been on this nonstop for two days already. Give yourself a break tonight. We'll call you when she's released."

"I'm staying. You can get a second agent if it makes you feel better, but I'm not leaving."

Dennis Johnson shook his head, not surprised by Kade's reaction. The ex-Special Ops soldier never backed down until a job had been completed. Johnson didn't know why he expected it would change tonight.

"All right, but I want her brought to headquarters the minute she's released. You understand?"

"Yes, sir." There was no trace of triumph in Kade's voice, just a bone-tired automatic response to the order of a superior.

Johnson took one more look at one of his best agents. "Get some rest."

Kade slumped into a chair and watched as Dennis walked toward the outside doors. Once closed, he rested his elbows on his knees and gripped his head with both hands.

How had tonight's surveillance of a bookish college student gone so wrong?

Chapter One

"If you'll sign here, we'll get Miss Sinclair ready." The young nursing unit clerk smiled at the handsome man who'd spent the night outside of the injured woman's room. She'd spotted him the moment she'd come on duty and hadn't been able to keep her eyes off him.

Kade signed the documents and passed them back across the counter, having no idea of the thoughts flashing through the hospital clerk's mind. "How long?"

She smiled up at him, hoping he'd note the interest in her eyes. "Not long, Mr. Taylor."

"Special Agent Taylor." Kade saw her welcoming smile, but didn't reciprocate. He'd seen the look all too often, knowing it for the trouble it was, and this young woman was none too subtle.

She nodded, scribbled on a piece of paper and folded it within the copies she handed back to Kade.

"I'll go check on her right now, Special Agent Taylor," she called over her shoulder as she walked toward Brooke's room. Within minutes she'd returned to her desk and her ongoing, not too subtle glances at Kade.

He paced toward the front windows, ready to get out of this place and start questioning Paco's girlfriend. She tried to play the serious graduate student but Kade suspected she knew quite a bit about her boyfriend's activities. With luck, they'd get the information needed for their investigation today and arrest her boyfriend before nightfall.

Kade looked outside and thought of Miss Sinclair's new, bright red SUV being searched by the tech team. No one else had been available, so he'd picked it up last night, parking his motorcycle at a friend's house. Vivian had been more than a little pissed when he'd shown up in the middle of the night, asking for a lift to the parking garage, then asking her to follow him to the impound garage. He'd have to make it up to her later.

Today, another tech team would be searching her apartment, checking for anything connecting her to the Bujazan family business. Between the two searches, he felt confident connecting evidence would turn up.

Kade turned to see a familiar figure walk through the double doors.

"Marshal Salgado. You here to help?"

"Moral support, my man." Ernesto Salgado held his hand out to his good friend. "But if you need back up..."

They turned at the sound of commotion coming from Brooke's room.

"What's going on?" Kade strolled into the room, stopping at the edge of the bed, in time to see a long, firm leg, before Brooke glanced up, saw him, and pulled the cover back over her semi-clothed body.

"Who are you?" She glared at him, folding her arms over her chest.

"I'm Agent Taylor with the DEA, and this is U.S. Marshal Salgado. We'll be taking you out of here."

"The hell you will. I'm not going anywhere with you."
She turned her attention to the nurse. "Where are my
clothes and belongings?"

"Agent Taylor signed for your belongings. Your
clothes are right here." The nurse picked up a clear plastic
zip bag and pulled out the contents before casting a
sympathetic glance at Kade.

"I told her she'd be leaving with a Federal Agent. She
didn't respond too well." The nurse glanced back at
Brooke with a stern gaze.

"Nurse, if you'd give us a minute, please?" Kade
asked, stepping aside as the nurse left the room.

"Miss Sinclair, you're part of an ongoing investigation
and I'm requesting you accompany me to headquarters
for questioning."

"What on earth are you talking about? Questioning
about what?" Brooke sat up and swung her legs off the
bed, immediately regretting it. She gripped the rolling
table for support, but it slid from her grasp. Kade
instinctively grabbed her arm to keep her from falling.

"Take it easy. You suffered a concussion in the
accident last night." He steeled himself from glancing
down at the long, shapely legs he'd only had a glimpse of
when he'd entered the room.

"What accident?" This time her eyes searched his, a
confused and painful look causing an immediate impact
on Kade. He stared for an instant before reclaiming his
composure.

Kade glanced at Marshal Salgado, who tried to hide a grin as he lowered his gaze.

"You walked into my motorcycle and fell, bumping your head on the pavement, then passing out."

"You? You're the one on the big black rocket who ran into me?" She reached for the phone. "I'm calling the police. You're the one who should be arrested."

Kade reached out and stilled her hand.

"Miss Sinclair, the questions won't take long and your input may help us to put some bad guys behind bars. You'll understand everything during questioning. Unless of course you'd rather we obtain a warrant for your arrest." Brooke shook her head enough to let Kade know a warrant wouldn't be necessary. He breathed a sigh of relief, knowing he'd never be able to get one given the lack of evidence. "The nurse will help you dress and we'll get out of here." Brooke started to protest before Kade held up his hand. "Miss Sinclair, it will be over before you know it."

Brooke assessed the situation. She had no one in San Diego she could call, but she did have her mother and stepfather in Arizona. "All right, but I want to make a phone call."

Kade and Ernesto shared a look.

"We need to get you out of this room, but you will have access to a phone at headquarters."

Kade's hard stare told Brooke the discussion had ended. She didn't like it but knew when to stay silent.

She'd call her stepfather, Heath MacLaren, and figure a way out of this horrible situation.

******

"Follow me, Miss Sinclair. I'll be taking you to see Senior Agent in Charge Dennis Johnson. He'll be questioning you." Kade placed his hand on her elbow, guiding her through the maze of hallways to an outside door, then led her into an open patio area. He'd provided a small amount of information to her on the ride over about the Bujazan cartel and Paco's connection to it. "We'll go to the building over there, where he'll meet you." He pointed to another building on the other side of a large patio.

"Wait, don't I get to make a phone call?" She moved away from Kade, still confused by the entire situation.

He glanced at his watch and led her back inside before grabbing her cell phone from the bag holding her belongings. "Here you go."

Brooke took the phone and dialed.

"Phyllis? Yes, it's Brooke. Is Heath available?"

Kade could see the look of disappointment on his Brooke's face.

"I see. Look, this is kind of an emergency. Let him know I need to speak with him right away." She looked at Kade. "Should he call me back on my phone?"

Kade provided his cell number, which she repeated to Phyllis. He wanted to know who she'd called.

10

"All right. Thanks, Phyllis, I really appreciate it."

She started to hand the phone to Kade, then pulled it back, looking at him. "Can I try one more number?"

"Make it quick."

She speed dialed a number and waited, praying it wouldn't go to voicemail.

"Cam, please just listen a moment and don't interrupt me. I was sideswiped by a motorcycle last night. They took me to the hospital, ran some tests, determined I was fine, and released me early this morning. The problem is a DEA agent brought me to their headquarters for questioning on a case they're investigating. They want to discuss what I might have seen, and question me about my friend. They think he's connected to some drug lord."

"That's enough, Miss Sinclair. We need to go."

Brooke turned from him, listening to her brother. "His name is Paco Bujazan. No, you don't have to fly out—" She fell silent, her head nodding at whatever was being said on the other end, and turned toward Kade. "He'd like to speak with you."

This wasn't what Kade had intended but he held out his hand. "This is Agent Kade Taylor. Who am I speaking to?" He jotted down the name. "I understand, Mr. Sinclair. Here is the number where you can reach me." He finished and handed the phone back to Brooke. "We need to go now, Miss Sinclair."

"Cam, I really must go." She listened another minute, seeing Kade's agitation grow and feeling a slight triumph. "Yes, I understand. Thanks. I love you." She ended the

11

call, and handed her phone back to Kade who slid it into the bag with her purse and other belongings.

"Let's go."

******

Kade watched through the one-way mirror as Dennis Johnson spoke with Brooke, still berating himself for allowing her another call when he knew his boss would be waiting. Kade didn't know Johnson's boss would also be attending the interrogation. He could see Brooke's confusion mount as they worked through the initial questions.

Kade felt his phone vibrate. He glanced at the Arizona prefix and decided to let it go to voicemail. It had to be either Cameron Sinclair, her brother, or the other man she'd called. Either way, he'd deal with it later.

"I have no idea what you're talking about. Paco is a friend, a fellow student, and nothing more."

Kade snorted at the lie. He'd followed the two of them for weeks and sat outside Paco's home late into the night on several occasions. She'd never stayed past one in the morning, but by the way she'd looked leaving the apartment, Kade knew they'd done more than study during her visits.

"I can't tell you what I don't know. His name is Paco Bujazan, he's from Mexico, and is a graduate student. We have the same advisor, Professor Krueger, but I'm sure you already have his name. Maybe he can give you more information." She sat back, clasping her hands in her lap, deciding she'd said enough.

Johnson and his boss pushed further. To everyone's disgust, she fell silent, refusing to answer any more questions until she spoke to a lawyer.

"All right, Miss Sinclair. We'll give you a few minutes to think over our questions." Both men stood and left, joining Kade to watch her reaction with them out of the room.

"What do you think, Taylor?" Johnson asked, noticing she sat remarkably still for someone who'd just been interviewed about a pending federal case.

"There's more going on with Bujazan than she's admitting. I checked her phone and they communicate several times a day, most calls lasting a few minutes. It's been going on since I started my surveillance."

"We'll have to keep digging." Johnson and his boss left to the continue questioning Brooke.

Kade watched the two men walk away, wondering if he had misinterpreted the relationship between Sinclair and Bujazan, then stopped himself. He'd learned not to second guess his conclusions. When he had in the past, he'd regretted it. The woman knew more about Paco's family and business dealings than she let on and even if it took days or weeks, they'd find out what they needed.

******

"I'm here to see Brooke Sinclair." Cameron reached into his pocket to pull out identification when he noticed a man dressed in jeans and leather jacket, hair pulled back in a queue, standing several feet away, staring at him. When the man made no move to walk over, Cam turned his attention back to the clerk who had busied herself checking the visitor log.

"Here she is. And your name?"

"Cameron Sinclair. I'm her brother." He turned at the sound of the sliding doors opening from the front entry where security checked everyone who came through the building. "Gus, thanks for coming." Cam held out his hand to Gustavo Hamilton Barker, a criminal defense attorney he hadn't seen since his last trip to San Diego.

"No problem. What's going on?" Gus glanced around and noted several agents standing in a couple of small groups. One in particular kept glancing in their direction.

"Like I said when I called, Brooke's being detained as a person of interest regarding an investigation involving her boyfriend. He's apparently connected to some drug family in Mexico."

"Do you have the boyfriend's name?"

Cam pulled a piece of paper from a pocket. "Bujazan. Paco Bujazan."

Gus looked around once more then grasped Cam by the elbow and led him several feet away. "Do you have any idea who the Bujazan family is?" Gus's voice had lowered to just above a whisper.

"Only what I was able to find in a quick Internet search."

"The family runs one of the biggest drug cartels in Mexico, which means they are a big supplier to the U.S. market. Francisco Bujazan is the head of the family, Paco is his son."

"Ah, hell." Cam scrubbed a hand over his face and cast another glance at the leather clad man who kept watching them. "There's no chance Brooke would be involved with someone like this Bujazan fellow, or anyone involved in drug trafficking." He took a deep breath.

"Mr. Sinclair?"

Cam walked over to the clerk, Gus close behind.

"She's being questioned now by Special Agent in Charge Dennis Johnson."

"This is her attorney, Gustavo Barker. He'll be accompanying me."

"Mr. Barker, may I have some identification?"

Within minutes, the two were escorted to a room where Brooke sat with the two DEA agents. The look of relief on her face when she saw Cam walk through the door would be an image he'd never forget.

"Brooke, how are you doing, honey?" Cam wrapped his arms around her, wanting nothing more than to walk out with her right now. He glanced at Gus. "Brooke, this is Gus Barker. He's an attorney I've known for a while. He's also a friend of Heath's."

"Miss Sinclair." Gus held out his hand to Brooke. "Let's try to find out what's going on."

15

Cam and Gus introduced themselves to Johnson and his boss.

"Our interview is over for now. However, we'd like you to stay in the area."

"Agent Johnson, my client will be happy to apprise you of her whereabouts, but unless you provide proof of an eminent arrest, you have no jurisdiction to dictate where she may travel at this time."

Johnson didn't like it and neither did his boss. However, they'd learned nothing from their conversation with Brooke, and had been notified by their tech teams they'd been unable to locate anything in her apartment or car connecting her to the Bujazan cartel. Johnson turned toward Brooke.

"Miss Sinclair, we would appreciate it if you would notify us of any trips you plan. This is not a requirement, just a request. Now, we'll leave the three of you alone."

Kade stood down the hall, a few doors away from where Brooke met with her brother and attorney. He wasn't too familiar with Gus Barker, but knew enough he wasn't happy when Barker walked through the doors. He had a clean reputation, primarily defending those charged with white collar crimes, not drug trafficking.

The DEA's intent had never been to obtain an arrest warrant. They wanted to scare Brooke enough she'd tell them everything Paco had disclosed to her, then they'd go after the big players, like Francisco Bujazan, and send the other associates, including Paco, back to Mexico or to jail.

16

"May we use a secure room for a while?" Gus asked Johnson before the agent closed the door.

"Follow me." Johnson led them down the hall to a room with glass toward the hall but without a two-way mirror—a room he assured them would be secure.

"It might save time if we talk here, rather than going to my office," Gus informed Brooke and Cam.

An hour later, Gus reviewed his notes.

"Let's go over this once more," Gus said. "You met Paco Bujazan several months ago when attending a function put on by your faculty advisor. Both of you are studying for doctorates in management. You're close to finishing, he has about a year left. Correct so far?"

"Yes." Brooke felt herself begin to relax, telling herself everything would be fine now that Cameron had arrived.

"You began to study together once or twice a week, but nothing more."

"It wasn't truly studying as you'd think of it. We shared ideas for our doctoral work, offered suggestions, listened to each other, and read and critiqued each other's work."

"When did you start seeing him more socially?"

"Several weeks ago, not long before mom had her accident." She looked at Cam, both remembering when their mother, Annie Sinclair MacLaren, had been hit by a drunk driver in Fire Mountain. "We'd meet for lunch or coffee. He suggested we change our meeting place to his home near the beach instead of trying to find a quiet

17

cubicle in the library. I met him there a couple of times before I got the call about mom. I went to Arizona and stayed for a week while mom recuperated. When I came back, Paco pushed for us to see each other more often, and, well, it seemed time for me to move on."

"Move on?" Gus asked.

"My fiancé and I had broken off our engagement quite a while ago. I'd stayed pretty closed until my family helped me see the time had come to get on with my life." Cam placed his hand on Brooke's and squeezed.

"Brooke, is there anything more to your relationship with Paco than friendship?"

"No. Absolutely not. We started having dinner a couple of times a week, sometimes we go to a movie, or study at his place. We also talk on the phone every day, sometimes several times a day." A sigh escaped her lips. "He has no family in the states, at least that's what he said. It can be lonely and hard to meet people on such a big campus."

Gus took notes, nodding once in a while.

"He never told you anything about his family, his father in particular?"

"He spoke little of his father and mother. He told me his father is a businessman in some type of import and export business. I never learned the exact products. His mother stays at home with the two smallest children, his oldest sister is married." Brooke pinched the bridge of her nose between her thumb and index finger. "I guess that isn't much, is it?"

18

"And you never knew he was related to the Bujazan cartel?"

"I didn't have a clue." She stood and paced to the back wall, turned and rested her head against it before closing her eyes. "Here I am a Ph.D. candidate and I wasn't smart enough to figure out Paco isn't who he seems." She opened her eyes in time to see Kade Taylor walk past the glass window of the room and glance inside. Her stomach twisted at the sight of him.

Cam noticed Brooke's grimace and turned to see the leather clad man walking slowly past their room, not hiding his interest in those inside.

"Who is that, Brooke?"

"Special Agent Kade Taylor. The man who ran me down with his motorcycle and dragged me into this mess."

Cam wasted no time pulling open the door and looking toward the agent. "I'd like a word with you Agent Taylor as soon as our visit with my sister is over."

"You must be the brother, Cameron Sinclair." Kade stopped a couple of feet away, sizing up the man who might be able to help their investigation. "You know, it would be best if you could get her to talk, tell us what she knows of the Bujazan operations and about Paco. What she's learned could go a long way in helping to close down the cartel."

Cam, being the president of a large business, had become an expert at reading people and their body language, and what he read from Kade Taylor told him much.

"You don't really have anything, do you Agent Taylor? It's all speculation, guilt by association, but no real substance, correct?"

"Right now your sister is a person of interest, nothing more. However, I assure you, if need be, we can get a warrant." Kade didn't need to defend himself to anyone, especially not a suspect's brother.

"I'm sure you must have run a thorough background check on Brooke. And if you did, you already know she hardly drinks, never does drugs, doesn't party, has few friends, studies way too much, and doesn't even have an outstanding parking ticket. She's as clean as anyone you'll ever meet. Now, what's your evidence someone like her would suddenly decide to throw everything, including her doctoral degree, out with the garbage to help the son of a drug lord?"

Kade glared at Sinclair, knowing he was right. They had little proof besides her frequent visits with Paco. "I can't share our evidence."

"Because you have none." Cam glanced through the window to see Brooke staring at him and Taylor. "Excuse me. We'll talk again—count on it."

Chapter Two

Brooke wanted to go home, take a bath, change clothes, and focus on anything except the hell she'd been through the last forty-eight hours. And, she never wanted to lay eyes on Special Agent Kade Taylor again.

"From everything you've told me, I can't find anything they could use to obtain an arrest warrant." Gus Barker flipped through his notes once more. "I believe you're what they indicated, a person of interest because of your friendship with Paco Bujazan. My suggestion is you stay as far away from him as possible until the investigation is complete. In fact, you may want to disassociate yourself from him entirely." They walked out into the hallway.

Brooke nodded, knowing she'd need to see Paco once more in order to explain why she had to distance herself from him. After all, neither he nor anyone in his family had been convicted of any drug trafficking crimes. Perhaps the DEA had their facts wrong.

"Agent Taylor, may I see you?"

Brooke, Cam, and Gus turned at the familiar voice to see Kade's boss standing down the hall.

Kade glanced toward Brooke, still with Cam and Gus, then at his boss.

"Yes, sir."

Brooke watched him leave, hopeful she would never see the man again.

"Come on. Let's get you home. I'll take you out to dinner." Cam wrapped an arm around her. "Gus, why don't you join us?"

"I'd like to, Cam, but I have plans. Brooke, I would like to meet with you again tomorrow morning at my office." He held out his card. "I'm sure I'll have a few more questions after reviewing my notes and would prefer to get everything down while it's fresh in your mind."

"Will eleven work? I have a meeting with my advisor at nine."

"Eleven is fine. I'll see you then."

"I'll be coming with her."

"You don't have to—" Brooke began.

"I'm staying, Brooke. I've already booked a room."

The men escorted her outside, Cam pointing to his rental car a couple of rows away. It was then Brooke spotted Kade Taylor, leaning against his black motorcycle, arms crossed, a smirk on his face. She was tempted to do something very unladylike, but instead, kept her anger in check. He wasn't worth the effort, she told herself as she slid into Cam's car.

"I'll see you tomorrow, Brooke." Gus shut the door and walked toward Kade. "I'm giving you notice, Agent Taylor. I'll be meeting with Assistant U.S. District Attorney Jeremy Flannigan. He and I have worked well together in the past. Once I provide him with what I've learned of Brooke and her relationship, or should I say lack of relationship, with Paco Bujazan, I'm certain you'll be turning to other sources for information to bring down the Bujazan cartel."

Kade watched Cam's car pull out before focusing on Barker. "Counselor, I do appreciate your insights. I hope you understand I have a job to do." He grabbed his helmet and secured it on his head before swinging his right leg over the motorcycle seat. "And I assure you, I will complete this investigation." Kade fired up the engine and started off. Neither he nor the agency were finished searching for answers which could bring down the Bujazan cartel. And Kade wasn't finished with his surveillance of Miss Brooke Sinclair.

******

"Is there anything else you can tell me, Brooke? Even if you believe it to be insignificant." Gus had taken several pages of notes, highlighting dates and times Brooke had met with Paco over the last few weeks.

"I can't think of anything. We don't talk about his family or mine much of the time. Our conversations focus on the topics for our dissertations, activities around campus, places we'd like to travel, future plans—the usual stuff."

"Did he talk about specific places he'd like to visit or travel plans?"

Brooke thought a moment, trying to recall the last place he'd mentioned. "Paco's talked about visiting a lot of places. I believe Hawaii may have been the last place he mentioned, and before that it was Canada."

"Does he ever talk about traveling to Central or South America?"

She rubbed the back of her neck, trying to clear her head and remember where else he wanted to visit. "I don't recall him ever mentioning anything south of the border besides visiting his family in Mexico. I'm sorry, I know it's not much."

"Neither of you have ever purchased anything relating to a trip together, right?"

"Right."

Gus sat back. They'd been at it for almost two hours without Brooke stumbling over any question he asked. Her answers were consistent no matter how he phrased each question. He'd sent a friend of his to Brooke's apartment earlier while she attended the meeting with her advisor. Cam let the security specialist inside and stayed with him as he scanned the apartment for any type of listening or monitoring devices. He found nothing.

"I have a meeting with Jeremy Flannigan, the Assistant U.S. District Attorney, tomorrow morning on another matter. We've worked together before and I've always found him to be reasonable. I'll be in touch," Gus said as they stood to leave.

"Where for lunch?" Cam asked as he and Brooke took the elevator to the street.

"Good local food or fancy?"

"Local, definitely."

Thirty minutes later they were seated at a restaurant located under the Coronado Bridge eating the best enchiladas Cam had ever tasted. He'd ordered three, plus rice and beans, and a Bohemia, telling himself he needed to run along the beach if he continued to eat this much. He watched as Brooke rested her head against the wall and closed her eyes.

"Are you okay?"

"I still have a headache from the accident. Nothing major, just annoying." Brooke's eyes moved to the door as a group of men walked in, all in suits except the last one who wore jeans and a leather jacket. Kade Taylor. "Oh no," she moaned, causing Cam to look behind him.

"Ah, your favorite Fed." Cam knew the man was doing his job, no matter how wrong the conclusions. "You ready to get out of here?"

"More than ready." Brooke threw her purse over her shoulder and turned in time to lock eyes with Agent Taylor. "Darn," she muttered when he broke ranks with his friends and walked toward her.

"Good afternoon, Miss Sinclair."

"Hello, Agent Taylor." She tried to move past him, but Kade cut off her retreat. "Excuse me, please." She tried again, this time he stepped aside.

"Anytime you want to meet and talk, let me know." He held out a business card.

Brooke looked over her shoulder at him. "You're kidding, right?"

"No, Miss Sinclair, I'm not." He moved closer, still holding out the card. "Take it. You never know when you might need to talk with someone."

She glanced at him then down at the card. "Fine, but don't expect to ever hear from me." Brooke grabbed it from his fingers and stuffed it into her purse, knowing she'd never use it. At least he backed off and rejoined his comrades.

Cam stood at the entry, watching the exchange and forcing himself not to interfere. He couldn't hear what Taylor said, or Brooke's response. Anyone watching would think they were two friends talking. He noticed Brooke take a card from Taylor's hand, then walk toward the exit.

"What was that about?"

"Agent Taylor wanted to give me his business card, in case I ever want to speak with him," she snorted, figuring the odds of ever needing to contact the arrogant federal agent were somewhere between zero and no chance.

Cam laughed, glad to see her beginning to relax. He hoped Gus would have good news for them tomorrow.

******

Kade stood next to his fellow agents and watched as Brooke slid into her SUV. She was a beauty. Not in the traditional sense of being considered stunning, more a girl-next-door attractiveness which drew people to her. He'd noticed it while watching her on campus interacting with other students and was certain she had no idea of how pretty she was or the effect she had on others. Her blond hair, blue eyes, and fit figure weren't uncommon in this region of California. He knew she worked out a few days a week and ran or walked along the beach. He found himself thinking if she weren't involved in this investigation, he'd like to pursue her in another way.

"Yo, Kade. You with us?"

He'd been so focused on Brooke he hadn't even noticed when Marshal Ernesto "Nesto" Salgado came up beside him and followed his gaze outside.

"Ah, I see you're checking out an item not on the lunch menu." Nesto grinned. He'd known Kade since before high school. Somehow they'd graduated, enlisted in the Army, made it into Special Ops training, lived through it, and both had chosen law enforcement careers. They'd each earned degrees in criminal justice while in the military. Kade wanted the excitement of undercover work available in the DEA. Nesto opted for the U.S. Marshal Service. Along the way, both had experienced plenty of fun times with the fairer sex, avoiding commitment in favor of adventure and adrenaline pumping jobs.

"The woman's a suspect, nothing more." Kade tore his eyes from the parking lot.

"Yeah, buddy, roger that." Nesto's voice contained a hint of sarcasm, enough to let Kade know his friend didn't believe it.

"How'd you get loose?" Kade asked as they joined a table with the other agents.

"I'm waiting for orders to transfer a prisoner from Colorado to California." Nesto took a large bite of his burrito.

"Anyone I know?"

"Hell, I don't even know who it is yet."

Kade looked at his friend's plate which overflowed with a burrito, two chili rellenos, three flautas, plus the obligatory rice and beans, and punched him on the arm.

"Slow down. You'll end up looking like your uncle Diego if you aren't careful."

Both grinned, remembering the man who'd raised Nesto—all three hundred pounds of him.

"Salgado, I heard you might jump ship and join a real law enforcement team." J.D. Montalban had come out of the Navy to join the DEA the same time Kade signed up. He, like Kade, worked undercover, although J.D. liked to consider his work a little more high class than Kade. Today he wore khakis and a polo shirt, typical attire for the assignments he worked.

"Sorry, Julius, but I get itchy just thinking about spending too much time south of our fluid border." The last type of assignment Nesto wanted was working undercover, up close and personal with the drug cartel establishment, J.D.'s specialty. "Besides, I don't speak the language, amigo."

"The hell you don't. You just don't speak it with the same flare."

Nesto grinned at his and Kade's friend. The three hung out together whenever they had a chance, which wasn't too often these days. Nesto started to send another barb in J.D.'s direction when his phone rang.

"Salgado," he answered, then stood and walked outside to take the call. "When? Sure, I've got it. Be there in twenty." He slid the phone back in his pocket as he walked back to the table and picked up his plate. "Business calls, gentlemen. Don't play too hard without me." He nodded at Kade and took off.

Kade watched him leave and wondered if maybe he should've made the same choice. With his education and service record, he could've gone DEA, Marshal Service, or any number of other state or federal agencies. He'd picked undercover work with the DEA for the adrenaline rush of working the streets and bringing in the worst of the drug traffickers. After several years working undercover though, he'd begun to tire of the lifestyle required for success. He'd promised himself to take a hard look at his job once this assignment ended and decide if a career adjustment might be in order. Kade would consider almost anything as long as a suit and tie weren't involved.

******

Cam sat at Brooke's dining room table, finishing his morning coffee and watching her pace back and forth, phone to her ear, talking to their mother. Annie Sinclair MacLaren had threatened for several days to fly out. So far they'd been successful in talking her out of it.

"Mom, really, I'm fine, and Cam is here. You're still on the mend and there's no reason to fly over here just to sit around with us. Besides, we expect to hear from Gus Barker today." She listened a moment, glancing at her brother and knowing he agreed with her about Annie staying in Fire Mountain. "All right, I'll tell him. Hugs to everyone. Love you, too." She hung up and let out a sigh.

"How's she doing?"

"Therapy is going well. Heath insists on taking her to the appointments with Dr. Newcastle." Brooke and Cam locked gazes, then started to laugh. Their mother had dated Dr. Newcastle for a brief time before Heath came to his senses and asked her to marry him. Heath had wanted her to find a different orthopedist after her accident, but in the end, he'd backed off, acknowledging Newcastle was the best choice.

"Heath is busy, of course, as is Eric." She walked to the table and sat opposite Cam. "Does Eric ever hear from Amber?"

Their younger brother worked as a director in the land acquisition and development division of the MacLaren Cattle Company. Amber had been Eric's high school and college sweetheart. The entire family thought they'd marry, until one of her professors had encouraged

30

her to move to New York to pursue her dream of acting on stage. She'd pleaded with Eric to go with her. He'd been too stunned and angry to even consider her request. He'd told her to make a decision between him and New York. She'd asked Eric several times over the following two weeks to reconsider, to try and work out a compromise. When he held firm, she made her choice. New York.

"I guess she still sends him an email once in a while, asking him the usual stuff, how he is, how the family is doing. He sends back short replies, not encouraging her yet not slamming the door. Honestly, I have no idea how he feels about her."

"I saw an ad in a magazine a few weeks ago and I'm certain Amber was the model."

Cam looked up from his computer screen. "No kidding. What kind of ad?"

"You wouldn't believe it if I told you."

"Try me."

"The ad featured her and an incredibly handsome man, holding the reins of two horses, and selling western wear."

"You mean like the Sheldon's Ranch Wear catalogue?"

"Exactly. You remember she grew up on a ranch in Colorado before her parents moved to California her freshman year. I have to say, she looked great." Brooke strode to a table and rifled through a stack of magazines, found the one she wanted, and started to flip through it. "Here it is." She showed it to Cam.

"Wow, she sure is a beauty. I wonder if Eric has seen this." He glanced at the ad once more before handing the magazine back to Brooke.

She tore out the ad and handed it to Cam. "You take it. Maybe you can find a way to get it in front of him."

Cam narrowed his eyes at her before a memory clicked. "That's right. You and Amber were pretty close. We all liked her, but you two hung out sometimes."

Brooke sat back down and rested her arms on the table. "I just wish Eric would've thought it through— talked with her about the options. She was crazy about him, you know."

Cam began to reply when Brooke's phone started to ring.

"This is Brooke." She looked at Cam and mouthed 'Gus' then continued to listen. "That's great news. Thanks so much for everything. Please send me a bill for what I owe you. All right, I'll tell him." Her beaming smile told Cam everything he needed to know.

"He had a good meeting with Flannigan?"

"Flannigan told Gus the investigation hadn't stopped and I'm just one of many people they are interviewing regarding the Bujazan family. If they found anything tying me to the Bujazan operations, they'd obtain a warrant. Gus recommended Flannigan consider focusing his resources somewhere else, as pursuing me would be a colossal waste of time," she smirked.

She could now resume her life, free from the constant surveillance by the handsome and completely annoying DEA agent.

"They searched your car and apartment, plus the desk you use at the university and found nothing. If they had, they'd already have a warrant. We both know there's nothing to find, and nothing to substantiate filing charges, so that's the end of it." He stood and walked around the table, pulling her into a comforting hug. She sank into him, resting her cheek against his chest, just as she'd done the day their father had passed away from his long illness. This time, however, they could celebrate.

Brooke dropped her arms and stepped back. "My turn to treat you to dinner tonight. How about Italian?"

"Italian it is."

******

"What do you mean I'm supposed to back off of tailing Miss Sinclair?" Kade sat forward in his chair and stared at Dennis Johnson.

"You heard me. Flannigan doesn't believe there's enough to continue focusing our resources on her. We thought there'd be something in her apartment or car, but we didn't find anything to tie her to Paco. She has no record and is a stellar student in the doctoral program. Flannigan believes we have more viable options."

"Well, hell."

"However, he doesn't have any say on how I run my department. In my mind, the investigation is ongoing. If we come up with anything implicating her, we'll go for a warrant."

Kade sat back and folded his arms across his broad chest. "Which means?"

"Watch her. Be subtle about it, don't let her spot your tail."

"How far do I take this?"

"Far enough until we can rule her out, but no more than a couple more weeks. I can't stretch our resources beyond then." Johnson glanced back down at the file. "You know, Kade, you may have to accept she isn't involved and move on. Paco is still the main focus."

"You already have Clive Nelson watching him." Kade stepped into the hallway, then turned at the sound of Johnson's voice.

"Just letting you know she might be as clean as her profile shows."

Kade pushed open the door toward the parking lot, irritated at the change in direction and still one hundred percent convinced Brooke played some part in the Bujazan business. He swung onto his chopper and pulled into traffic, replaying the events of the last month. She'd seen Paco a couple dozen times, including twice a week at his home, yet they hadn't found anything to tie her to Paco's family. What was it he and his team were missing?

Half an hour later he pulled into Vivian's driveway. She didn't work tonight which gave him plenty of time to properly thank her for the ride a couple of nights before to pick up Brooke's car. The one night stand he'd planned with Vivian had turned into two months. He knew the time had come to call it off, no use letting her believe more would come of it. The problem seemed to be comfort. She made no demands, always welcomed him, and never called between visits. The perfect set up, yet somehow it seemed like just another black hole he was trying to claw his way out of.

Chapter Three

Brooke gave Cam one more hug before he boarded the MacLaren plane for Fire Mountain.

"Thanks for being here." Her voice cracked. Cam and their younger brother Eric had always been there for her, lending support, and providing advice. Now she had the support of her stepfamily also.

"Eric wanted to come out but I told him to wait. He's in the middle of finishing up a preliminary review of a potential acquisition that's been put off too long already." Cam started up the steps and turned back. "Why don't you come home, Brooke? You can work on your thesis presentation and spend time with the family. It might be good for you."

Brooke had been thinking the same thing. She needed a break and the timing was perfect.

"You may be right. Let me talk to my faculty chair and I'll call you."

She stayed on the tarmac as the jet taxied down the runway, waited, then started its ascent. Her thesis had been completed weeks before, leaving her the task of preparing to defend it before her faculty chair and committee. Visiting Fire Mountain now wouldn't hinder her progress in any way, and in fact, might give her the jolt she needed to reclaim her motivation.

Brooke shoved both hands into her pockets and walked through the gate toward the parking area. She'd speak with her faculty advisor, let her neighbors know she'd be gone, and pack. If all went well, she could arrive at the ranch within a few days.

******

Kade sat on his motorcycle, hidden between some parked cars, and watched Brooke climb into her SUV. She sat a couple of minutes before pulling onto the busy street which fronted the airport on one side and the bay on the other. He followed at a discreet distance, maneuvering his chopper around traffic to keep her in sight.

Paco had left the day after his last meeting with Brooke for a visit with his family, leaving a message on her voicemail canceling a date they had planned. The tech team had listened to it during the search of her apartment, noting Paco hadn't given any information about his return.

A hunch began to form in Kade's mind. An idea he and his colleagues hadn't discussed before, but now seemed the most plausible explanation for Paco's interest in Brooke. The agency knew he had a girlfriend in Mexico, one he saw during each of his visits home. Perhaps Paco's interest in Miss Sinclair stemmed from a need to use her as a go-between with someone else. If so, then who? Brooke had few friends besides Paco and her trips consisted of errands to the store and the university. She had no social life from what they could tell.

An image of her popped into his head. She'd flashed Nesto and him a look of shock and pure defiance when they'd entered her hospital room, informing her she was a person of interest in an investigation. Even in pain, angry over the announcement, and tired from a sleepless night, Brooke Sinclair had to be one of the most attractive women Kade had ever seen. He'd felt drawn to her, as if some mystical magnetic force pulled them together. He'd been glad to deposit her at headquarters for questioning, although he'd struggled with a continuing need to check on her. She radiated a sense of strength and determination, while at the same time showing a vulnerability which tugged at him.

A horn blast from a side street drew his attention, and he let his thoughts of Brooke slide from his mind.

He followed her until she pulled into a spot outside the location of her advisor's building. Another meeting. Well, he'd relax and wait, and think through how Bujazan Junior might be passing information between himself and someone else using Brooke as the unsuspecting courier. Even though drug trafficking was the Bujazans main business, the agency had long suspected the family of aiding terrorists who wanted to cross into the United States. And they had no reservations about using naïve, law-abiding citizens to further their cause.

******

Fire Mountain, Arizona

"Welcome back. " Heath MacLaren, CEO of the MacLaren Cattle Company, walked around his desk and shook hands with his youngest stepson, Eric Sinclair. "Tell me about Montana."

Eric had spent the last week in Crooked Tree, home of RTC Bucking Bulls, a thriving business Heath and his brother Jace had a strong interest in acquiring. The company raised some of the finest bucking stock for the rodeo circuit, made consistent profits, and had a clean reputation. The acquisition would fit well with their recent purchase of a bucking horse business in Colorado, where Cam served as president.

"Crooked Tree seems like a good town and RTC is about as solid an operation as we'll find. I'm not the expert, you and the others are, but from what I saw, it's definitely worth pursuing."

"Did you meet all three partners?"

Eric glanced at his stepfather, well aware of the issues if they moved forward. The company was equally owned by three partners, Rafe, Ty, and Chris, good friends since high school. Ty and Chris wanted out. They'd spent a lot of years building the business and wanted to take their profits and retire, or try their luck in another venture. Rafe didn't feel the same.

Chris and Ty had contacted Heath and his brother, Jace, confidentially, about a possible sale. The one issue everyone knew could stop the sale at any time was a subject they rarely spoke about. Rafael 'Rafe' MacLaren was the estranged middle brother of Heath and Jace.

"I did. First with Ty and Chris, then later with Rafe, although I spent little time with him. He knows his partners are talking to potential buyers, and I'll tell you, he isn't inclined to be cooperative. I believe he's hoping nothing will come of it and they'll back off."

Heath inhaled a deep breath. He hadn't seen Rafe since he'd stormed from their home before Trey MacLaren, Heath's son, was born. Their father had died not long afterwards. Jace and he hadn't heard a word from him since, even though they'd tried to locate Rafe. Years later, they learned he and a couple high school friends had started RTC in Montana. Heath and Jace wanted to work through their issues and offer him his place in the MacLaren businesses. This could be either the start of a reconciliation or an irreversible failure.

"I'll get with Doug and Colt. Colt will have his partner travel to Crooked Tree in his place. Rafe and Colt knew each other before Rafe left Fire Mountain. We need to be careful until we've made a final decision. No sense stirring up more trouble between the partners than already exists."

Heath had a lot of faith in his CFO, Doug Hester, and their outside attorney, Colt Minton, who had handled the major legal affairs of MacLaren Cattle Company for years. The two were part of a team which now included Cam and Eric whenever Heath and Jace wanted to evaluate a potential acquisition.

"If they give their approval..." Eric's voice trailed off as he waited for Heath's response.

"We'll send Cam."

"How will you and Jace deal with Rafe if Cam gives the thumbs up?"

Heath stood and walked to the large picture window that looked out onto hundreds of acres of MacLaren land. Land belonging to three brothers, not just him and Jace.

"I honestly don't know how we'll handle it, Eric." He turned back toward his stepson. "Somehow, we will make it all work out."

******

"I can't stay long, Paco." Brooke took a seat in her usual chair in the spacious living room which looked out over the Pacific Ocean. She had to find a way to bring up the subject that vexed her since the appearance of Agent Taylor—Paco and his family's association with the drug trade.

"Are you leaving tomorrow?"

"After I see Professor Krueger in the morning."

"How long will you be gone?" Paco reached for his glass of wine and took a slow sip, watching Brooke over the rim.

"Two weeks tops."

"It's always good to spend time with family," Paco said, his mind sorting through options. "Are you sure you don't want some wine?"

She looked at his glass. "Wine does sound good." She'd get some wine then ask him straight out about the Bujazan family.

Paco began to rise before Brooke stood and started for the kitchen.

"I can get it. Be right back."

He watched her close the kitchen door then reached for her notebook. She used one her father had given her with a thick leather cover and the three rings common in traditional binders. She refused to use anything else. Paco pulled a slim object, the size of a credit card, from his pocket. He slid it into a concealed slit in her binder then pinched the ends together, sealing the object inside. The kitchen door swung open as he finished.

"I hope it's all right to look at your most recent notes." He settled back into the sofa, crossed a leg over one thigh, and held the open notebook in front of him. "I'm curious as to the direction you'll take with your conclusions."

"Of course it's all right. Your comments are always welcome." Instead of taking her usual spot, Brooke slid next to him in order to read over his shoulder. She'd told him the short version of her questioning, not mentioning the DEA or the charges, only the fact everything had been dropped.

"Tell me more about what happened when you were questioned. I wish I'd been here, maybe I could have helped."

"They were DEA agents, Paco."

Paco set down his glass and crossed his arms. "Go on."

"They asked me what I know about you and your family."

His eyes narrowed on her. "Why would they ask you such questions?"

Restless, Brooke stood and paced toward the other side of the room. "They told me your family is involved in drug trafficking and you're part of the operation. They believe I have knowledge of what's going on." She fixed her gaze on him. "Is it true?"

Brooke didn't need to ask. She'd done her own research and found a wealth of information about the Bujazan family, much of it not flattering. However, nothing she read indicated anyone in the family had ever been convicted of the crimes Special Agents Johnson and Taylor mentioned.

He pushed from the sofa and walked toward her. She backed up a few inches, a sense of unease building.

"No, it isn't true, but the United States government believes otherwise and has made our lives miserable. We own import and export businesses, plus a few other smaller companies. All legal." He took a few more steps until he stood before her. He raised a hand and let his knuckles graze a path down a cheek, over her jaw, and down her neck before stepping away. "You believe me, right?"

She glanced around the spacious living room of a house she knew cost millions. Of course, families with legal businesses could afford this type of luxury, except now, doubts had entered her mind. She needed to get away and think.

"Of course. I told them I knew little of your family, except they own businesses and live in Mexico. There wasn't much to tell them."

He watched her eyes, knowing she truly did know nothing of his family except the brief pieces of information he'd fed her. All of it about his mother or siblings. No details at all about the businesses.

Paco turned and strode back to the coffee table, picked up his glass, and finished his wine.

"Well, it's over now." He offered a vague smile. Brooke didn't know what to think, except, she needed time away. Perhaps she could get her life back on track at the ranch, surrounded by family, and the calming landscape of the region.

Paco changed the subject to his own thesis and the progress he'd made, as well as the small amount of research he'd done while visiting his family.

"Was it a good trip for you?" Brooke asked, now more curious than ever about his family.

"What can I say? I go when they call, but the whole time I think of you."

Brooke laughed, knowing he made too much of their friendship. He'd kissed her twice, both times fleeting and with little passion. She'd felt nothing either time.

44

Although she enjoyed Paco's company, there'd never been the spark other friends spoke about. Of course, she'd never felt a spark with her ex-fiancé, Perry, either.

The only time she'd ever felt anything more for a man was when the obnoxious DEA agent, Kade Taylor, had been close. Her body responded in inexplicable ways when he was around—her chest would tighten, her heart would race, and she'd feel an odd sensation in her stomach. She'd never felt anything like this with her ex-fiancé. It confused and maddened her.

For a well-educated woman, she found herself almost tongue tied when the imposing agent stood anywhere near. When he'd led her from one place to another with his hand on her elbow or the small of her back, she'd felt an almost comforting jolt of recognition. None of it made sense, considering he wanted to see her behind bars.

******

Kade, and Clive Nelson, the agent in charge of following Paco, sat in a local bar several blocks from the university. Each had watched Brooke enter the Bujazan residence then leave over an hour later, returning to her apartment. Clive had been the one to insist Brooke had to be involved and Kade had let his arguments sway him. Yet it had been their boss's call to approach Jeremy Flannigan for approval to pick up Miss Sinclair for questioning and warrants to search her property. Now

Kade found himself in the position of defending her, knowing it wouldn't set well with the other agent.

"Look Clive, your surveillance of Paco won't change until we've closed the door on the Bujazan empire. I've been given a couple more weeks to link Miss Sinclair to the family, then Johnson will pull me. We're at a standstill unless I can catch her with more than your gut feeling." Kade took a long draw from his bottle of beer and sat back.

"I thought the searches would turn up something. What did I miss?" Clive asked.

"She may be just what she seems—a Ph.D. student with no ties to Paco other than being a fellow student."

"That's crap and you know it. Bujazan Junior doesn't make friends unless they'll further the company's business. There's a reason he spends so much time with Sinclair." Clive thought through the connections again before locking eyes with Kade. "Shit," he muttered when the obvious became apparent. "He's using her as a courier."

"That's what I think. We found nothing during the searches, which means anything he gives her must be hidden in the normal items she uses every day."

"Her purse?"

"We didn't find anything. Besides, I doubt she'd leave her purse lying around for someone to rifle through."

"The only other items she carries are books."

Kade slammed his hand against the wooden counter. "Her notebook. She takes it everywhere, including all her visits with Paco. He must be slipping the package inside."

"Who retrieves it?"

"My guess is someone at the university. They would need access to the notebook for a minute or two to retrieve whatever Paco might put inside."

"You realize all of this is conjecture." Clive took another swig of his beer.

"We work on hunches, my friend. At this point, it's the best I've got to explain his interest in Brooke."

"What next?"

"The next time she visits the university, I'll follow her inside. We know she went from Paco's home to her apartment tonight. Unless someone breaks into her place, the first chance of a contact retrieving the information is tomorrow."

"She doesn't know me. I should be the one tailing her inside." Clive knew he'd have the best chance of following her into the university building without being detected.

"What about Paco?"

"He spends most of his time at the university anyway, in the same building. Odds are he'll already be on campus when Miss Sinclair shows up."

Clive stood and threw a few dollars on the bar before exiting out a back door.

Kade finished his beer and ordered one more, taking time to think through the plan to follow Brooke. With luck, she'd stop by the school tomorrow so they could check their theory. If not, it could be a long few days.

******

"My guess is I'll be on the road before ten and at the ranch before supper." Brooke cradled the phone between her ear and shoulder as she pulled the rolling bag toward her car and lifted it inside. "I'll call when I leave San Diego. Love you too, Mom."

She'd make a quick stop at the school to see Professor Krueger and then be on her way. She pulled onto the street, not noticing the gun metal grey truck parked a few cars away.

"She's moving." Kade spoke into his headset with Clive on the other end. "I'll let you know her destination."

He stayed close behind, knowing within minutes where she was headed, which he reported to Clive.

"Already here." Clive watched for the red SUV. Within minutes Brooke parked in the lot. He watched her pull the leather binder from the car before walking inside and was tailing her within seconds. "I've got her," he said into his microphone, following her up a flight of stairs and down a hall.

"Good morning, Nancy. Is he in?" Brooke asked the department assistant.

"Hi, Brooke. Not yet, but I expect him soon."

"I'll be at my desk. I just need a couple minutes of his time."

48

Brooke turned down another hall and disappeared from Clive's view as a group of students walked toward him. He joined the back of the group, passing Nancy's desk, and following them as they took the same route as Brooke. He spotted her in a small cubicle as she laid her notebook down and pulled a few papers from it. Clive continued another few feet and ducked into an empty cubicle next to hers.

"Brooke? Dr. Krueger just walked in if you want to catch him before anyone else shows up."

"Thanks, Nancy." Brooke grabbed the papers she needed and dashed down the hall behind Nancy, knocking on Krueger's door and vanishing inside.

Clive waited a couple of minutes before hearing someone in her cubicle. He walked toward her desk to see a slender male, about Brooke's age, pick up her binder, turn it over, as if searching for something, fingering a seam on the bottom. He dropped it when Clive appeared.

"Is Brooke around?" Clive asked, taking a good look at the slender man, whose eyes darted around nervously.

"She's not here right now." His voice shook as he started to move around Clive, who blocked his path to the hall.

"I can see that. Do you know if she's in the building?"

"Uh, no, I'm not sure." He tried once more to get past Clive.

"Are you waiting for her also?" Clive asked, seeing the tension in the man's face escalate.

"No, just dropping something off. Look, I need to get going."

Both men turned at the sound of Brooke's voice. The man took the opportunity to slide past Clive and dash the opposite direction from where Brooke stood in the doorway of Krueger's office.

"Thanks, Dr. Krueger. I'll give you a call next week once I get your suggestions."

Clive ducked back into his cubicle and out of sight. He glanced over the top divider enough to see Brooke grab her notebook and take off.

"Nancy, I'll be out of town for a couple of weeks."

"Vacation or work?" Nancy asked.

"Visiting my family in Arizona."

"I have your phone number and email if Dr. Krueger needs it. Have a great time, Brooke."

"Thanks, Nancy. I plan to."

Clive followed her outside, adjusting his ear bud. "She's on her way outside, and get this, she's headed to visit her family in Arizona."

"What?"

"You heard me. Someone tried to retrieve an item from the binder she left on her desk. I didn't recognize him. Slender male, about five foot eight inches tall, brown hair. He dashed out the back when I interrupted him."

"Did he get anything?"

"No, but he was after something, Kade, and he didn't want her to see him."

"Here she comes. I've got her from here."

Brooke took her time climbing into her SUV. She pulled out her phone and Kade could see her talking before she hung up and started the engine. She turned onto the main road, but instead of heading south toward the airport, she drove north, then took the connecting freeway east until it hit the interstate toward San Bernardino. He needed to let Clive know.

"What's going on?" Clive asked when he saw the caller I.D.

"She's headed out of town all right, but not by air. She's driving."

"You've got to locate what the guy was after, Kade."

"I will."

"Hope you filled up your tank. Hold on a minute."

Kade could hear Clive close a car door. "I followed Paco to his home a few minutes ago and guess who just showed up."

"The guy you saw in Brooke's cubicle."

"Bingo."

"Are you getting pictures?"

"Already done. I'll send them to headquarters. With luck we'll have him identified soon. Keep me posted on Miss Sinclair." He clicked off.

Kade kept a respectable distance between his truck and Brooke's car, guessing her destination to be the town her brother, Cameron Sinclair, lived. He settled into the seat, reached behind him to grab a bottle of water from the back, and reconciled himself to the fact he'd be in Fire Mountain, Arizona before nightfall.

******

"What do you think you're doing, coming to my home? You are never to come here. Ever." Paco Bujazan couldn't contain the anger he felt at seeing Perry Worton pounding on his front door. He'd let his bodyguards allow the man inside, the same bodyguards who stayed hidden whenever Brooke had visited.

"There's a problem." Perry moved further into the room, ignoring the muscle posted near Paco. He scrubbed a hand over his perspiration soaked face and dropped into a chair. "I didn't get the package. Some guy interrupted me just before Brooke walked out of Krueger's office. I had to take off or she would've seen me."

"You're telling me the package is still in her possession?" Paco ground out, anger obvious in his tone.

Perry looked up and nodded, and once again realized the danger surrounding him. No one knew of his association with the cartel. He'd made a mistake a year before and now he'd be paying for it the rest of his life.

"So you failed." Paco turned from him and paced toward the massive picture window.

"It was just the one time. I've made all the other exchanges to your contact."

"This one, Mr. Worton, held information essential to our business operations. It would be most unfortunate if it fell into the wrong hands."

Perry's eyes darted between Paco and his bodyguards. "I'm sorry."

"Sorry is not enough. The package must be retrieved and given to our contact." He walked to within a foot of Perry and stared down at him. "You, Mr. Worton, will recover the package and deliver it as we agreed." Paco looked to one of his men and reached into his pocket. "Julio, you will meet Mr. Worton at this address in one hour and accompany him to make certain he does not forget what he is after." He turned back to Perry and handed him the same address. "Do we understand each other, Mr. Worton?"

Perry rubbed his eyes and stood. "Yes, we understand each other, Mr. Bujazan."

Chapter Four

"It's good to have you home." Eric, Brooke's younger brother, wrapped her in a hug. "We've been worried about you." He dropped his arms and grabbed her suitcase from her SUV. "I'll bring this. Go ahead and say hi to everyone."

She didn't have to walk far before being engulfed by her mother, Heath, Cam, and his wife, Lainey.

"We're so glad you came home." Annie gave her daughter a hug, then stepped away so the others could have their turn.

"This is the exact place I want to be after this last week."

"Cam told us most of it. Come on inside and you can fill in the missing pieces." Heath wrapped an arm around his stepdaughter's shoulder as they walked inside and took seats in the large great room. "What can I get you to drink?"

"Ice tea would be perfect, if you have it." Brooke continued standing as she looked around the room which hadn't changed since her last visit. Over six hours in the car had left her muscles stiff and a little sore so she welcomed the opportunity to stand and stretch.

"Here you are." Annie handed her a glass. "Has anything happened since Cam left?"

"No, nothing. I made the decision when Cam came home to drive over here as soon as I could. Dr. Krueger knows how to reach me."

"Nothing from Special Agent Taylor?" Cam asked.

"Not a thing. I'm glad to get the egotistical pain in the ass out of my life. Sorry, Mom."

Annie shrugged, knowing her daughter needed to work through her frustrations.

Brooke sat on the arm of a large easy chair and sipped her tea. "I know he followed me from the airport after Cam's plane took off. I almost called Gus, then decided to wait and see if he showed up again today, but I saw no sign of him. I'm hoping he's finally out of my life."

"What did he do to set you off?" Lainey asked. "Was he rude or rough with you?"

Brooke scrunched her face and shook her head. "Nothing like that. He was…I don't know. Exasperating. There was something about him that had me on edge. Didn't you feel it, Cam?"

"Nope, can't say I did." He shot his wife an amused look getting a quick nod from Lainey in return. "He seemed like any other lawman to me, just doing his job."

Eric watched the exchange, the corners of his mouth turning up, although he remained silent. Brooke was smart, brilliant in some ways, yet still naïve in others.

"Well, I found him irritating." She rubbed the back of her neck and twisted it from side to side, trying to get the kinks out. "I'd get a strange prickly feeling whenever he was around. It was maddening." She finished off her tea and looked toward her mother. "Do you need some help with dinner?"

"No, honey. It'll only take a minute to get it all on the table. Heath, do you mind carrying the casserole to the table?"

"Not at all." Heath followed Annie to the kitchen, knowing she didn't need help, but going along with her request. "What was that about?"

"It appears to me Special Agent Taylor made a strong impression on Brooke. And not all bad, either."

"She seems adamant about never wanting to see him again. What am I missing?" Heath picked up the large serving platter and looked over his shoulder at his wife.

"Call it a mother's intuition if you want, it just seems her protests are a little too strong. For whatever reason, I'm not convinced she wants to be rid of Special Agent Taylor."

******

Kade followed Brooke until she started down a long private drive. Trailing her onto the property wasn't an option, his truck would be too easy to spot, but at least he knew where she'd be staying. He noted the numbers on the fence and decided to call it a day.

It took about twenty minutes to find a motel, register, and get settled in a room. Nothing fancy, a couple of queen size beds, desk, television, and not much else. He threw his wallet and keys on a table, fell back onto the bed and dialed his boss's number.

"Johnson."

"It's Kade. I'm in Fire Mountain." He gave Dennis Johnson the name of the motel and his room number. "I need someone to check an address and let me know who it belongs to."

"Go ahead."

Kade rattled off the route number, and the number on the fence. "That's all I have."

"It should be enough. What about the notebook?"

"I didn't see it, but my guess is she has it with her. I'll know more tomorrow after I've checked out the property. I couldn't get a good look from the road, but my sense is this won't be some small nondescript home in the mountains."

Johnson snorted. "It's never that easy. Look, I'll check out the address and let you know what I find."

"Thanks." Kade tossed his phone on the bed as his stomach started to growl. He'd grabbed a couple of energy bars earlier when Brooke stopped for gas, but those had worn off long ago. Now he needed real food to fill him up.

Within minutes he parked in an area populated by restored buildings, small boutiques, neighborhood bars, and restaurants. It reminded him somewhat of where he'd grown up in Montana. He spotted a sports bar advertising food and found an empty stool as his phone rang.

"Taylor."

"Where are you?" Clive's booming voice could be heard even over the sports announcers on the various television screens.

"At a bar in Fire Mountain. What's up?"

"Trouble. Someone called in a burglary at Miss Sinclair's apartment and one of our team members heard about it. I'm here now." Kade could hear him blow out a breath. "It's bad, Kade. Someone tore her place apart."

"Shit," Kade muttered.

"They must be after whatever she has with her."

"Any idea who did it?"

"From the neighbor's description, it appears our boy from earlier today might be the one. I should have an I.D. back on him anytime, but he fits. The lady next door got a pretty good look at him."

"That means Paco doesn't know she left town."

"That's my guess."

"Does he know where her family lives?"

"Don't know, Kade, but you'd better assume he does. I just wanted to let you know. For now it's considered a police matter, but I need to let Johnson know." Clive stopped a moment to speak with someone else, then got back on the line. "I told the police we'd be in touch with Miss Sinclair about her apartment. The neighbor has her number but was too shaken up to call. I asked her to hold off until we'd had a chance to speak with her."

"Got it. Get back to me when you have an I.D."

"Will do."

Kade needed to rethink his plan. The situation had taken a major detour with the tossing of her place. Whatever she had must be worth a great deal to Paco. From what Kade could tell, Brooke had no idea she'd been used as a pawn.

Now he had to inform her of the break-in at her apartment. He knew she'd want to return to San Diego right away which meant he'd have to find a way to stall her. Kade didn't believe it was a coincidence her place had been trashed the day she'd disappeared with whatever Paco had slipped into her notebook. He was certain the two incidents were related, he just needed to find out how.

What if she'd been home? The question flashed across his mind without warning and Kade felt a shiver run up his spine, a reaction he'd never felt in the past when a suspect's property had been violated. He shook it off, deciding his reaction had nothing to do with the attraction he felt toward her and everything to do with his lack of food and sleep. He'd finish eating, crash at the motel, and visit Miss Sinclair early tomorrow.

******

"What's got you up so early?" Eric strolled into the kitchen at six the next morning, having stayed at the main house instead of his cabin several miles away.

"It's such a gorgeous day I thought I'd go for a ride. Do you want to join me?"

"Sounds great. I'll let Mom and Heath know."

By seven o'clock, they'd ridden a couple of miles from the ranch, heading toward the mountains to the northwest and a lookout point with incomparable views.

"What's Heath got you working on now?" Brooke asked as they made their way to the top of a nearby hill an hour later.

"Another possible acquisition. This time in Montana."

"What type of business?"

"Bucking bulls. If we go ahead with it, my thought is Heath may hold up on anything else for a while." Eric reined his horse to a stop. "I think he's picked up a rock."

"I'm ready to take a break anyway. It's been a while." She slid off her horse and stretched, feeling her back muscles ease. "Have you flown there to check it out?"

"Just got back a few days ago. Heath's sending the CFO and attorney up next week. If they give their okay, Cam will be the next one to go."

"Why don't Heath or Jace fly up there?"

Eric dropped the horse hoof and stood, glancing at Brooke as he wondered how to explain the delicate situation.

"It's complicated. He and Jace are familiar with one of the three partners, and he happens to be the only one not interested in selling. Do you remember Heath ever mentioning their third brother?"

"Rafael or Rafe, right?"

"Good memory. Neither Heath nor Jace has seen or spoken with him since before Trey was born. Guess who the third owner is?" Eric grabbed a bottle of water and gulped down half.

"Oh no."

"Small world. So, instead of Heath and Jace taking the lead, they have the rest of us providing our input. Cam, Doug, and Colt did the due diligence on the bucking horse business in Colorado, and the purchase went through without a hitch. I'm the only one new to the process."

"It's great experience for you. Have you met Rafe?"

"I have and I like him. He isn't keen on selling but he's agreed to talk to a few buyers to evaluate their options. I sat in his office. Rafe has one wall full of pictures of his family. I believe he said there are five kids. All grown and out of the house. It was eerie looking at the photos of people who resembled Heath and Jace."

"And not being able to say anything."

"Right. The interesting part is, if you take certain aspects of Heath and Jace, you'd get Rafe."

"As I recall, he had a different mother, and he's between the other two in age."

"Their mom and dad separated for a while after Heath was born. He hooked up with some other woman before reconciling with his wife. Rafe is the result. When Rafe's mother died, the MacLarens moved him right into the house and treated him no different than Heath and Jace."

"But they had a falling out."

"The father and Rafe did, and by association, Heath and Jace, who sided with their father. I don't know specifics, but Rafe took off in a huff and never came back."

"Well, it seems he did all right for himself."

"That he has. Ready to ride?"

"Sure am."

******

"I'm Special Agent Kade Taylor. Is Miss Sinclair at home?" Kade stood outside, still reeling from the name of Brooke's stepfamily. Dennis Johnson called earlier with the specifics about who owned the property—Heath and Jace MacLaren.

"Good morning, Agent Taylor. Please, come in. I'm Annie MacLaren, Brooke's mother." Annie stepped aside to let him pass. "Brooke and her brother, Eric, are out on a ride, but I'll get my husband. May I get you anything to drink?"

"No, I'm fine ma'am."

"All right. Make yourself comfortable. I'll be right back."

He looked around the spacious entry which opened into a huge great room on one side and a study on the other. Kade found himself drawn to a wall of photos in the study. He looked at each one, then stopped when he came across one with an image of a man he'd never met but recognized.

"That's a photo of me and my brothers. It was taken many years ago and is one of the few I have with all three of us together." Heath stood next to Kade as they both focused on the picture of three young men and their horses. "I'm Heath MacLaren. What can I do for you?" He extended a hand which Kade shook.

"I need to speak with Brooke, but I understand she isn't available."

"We expect her back soon. Is there anything we can help you with?" Heath gestured to a couple of chairs as Annie walked in with a tray of coffee.

"I know you said you didn't want anything, but I already had the coffee made."

"Thank you, ma'am." Kade grabbed a mug, added some cream and took a seat. "I suppose she told you about the last week."

"I believe you played a big role in the adventure." Annie settled next to Heath and waited for the agent's response.

"I suppose that's true. It's a tricky situation—more dangerous than we first thought."

Heath leaned forward, his gaze locking on Kade's. "In what way?"

"We now believe Brooke is unknowingly being used as a courier for the Francisco Bujazan cartel. And, we believe she currently has in her possession some information critical to our investigation. However, the bigger issue right now is someone ransacked her apartment last night, looking for the information."

"The DEA?" Annie asked.

"Not us. Whoever broke in trashed the place, turned everything upside down, slit open her mattress, and emptied her closets. I haven't seen it, but I've been told they were quite thorough."

"My God." Annie placed a hand over her mouth, her eyes wide.

Heath looked at his wife. "She'll want to go back."

"It's the last place she should be right now. There's nothing she can do and it might put her in danger. A neighbor saw the intruder and the description matches someone we suspect of being involved with Paco Bujazan, Francisco's son." Kade set his cup down. "I need your help convincing her to stay here."

"Of course, we'll do what we can. But the final decision will be up to her." Heath grabbed the coffee pot and topped off his cup. "Is there any chance they know she's here in Fire Mountain?"

"We must assume they know her location."

They turned at the sound of laughter coming from the entry.

"Brooke, we're in here," Annie called.

She broke into another round of laughter at a comment Eric made then came to an abrupt halt when her eyes landed Agent Taylor.

"We meet again, Miss Sinclair." Kade stood and walked toward her, taking in the sight as his chest tightened. Something about Brooke made his body go off track each time he saw her and he couldn't seem to control the reaction.

Brooke stood erect, her chin jutting out, doing her best to quell the pulsing sensation of blood rushing through her veins.

"Agent Taylor. To what do I owe the pleasure?" Her gaze wandered over him. In contrast to the other times she'd seen him, he wore tan khakis with a deep brown shirt, which set off his warm, olive-toned complexion. She looked down to see what appeared to be hand-tooled cowboy boots. As always, his long hair had been pulled back and tied with a leather string, and she found herself wondering what it would feel like loose with her fingers running through it.

"I need to speak with you."

She looked behind him at her mother and Heath.

"They already know why I'm here." He turned toward the man Brooke was with and extended his hand. "I'm Special Agent Kade Taylor."

"Eric Sinclair."

They took seats and Kade described once again what had happened in Brooke's apartment, trying his best to not alarm her, knowing he couldn't avoid it.

"My God. I've got to go back." Brooked jumped from her chair.

"That's the last place you should be right now." Kade's deep, steady voice stopped her. She swung around and glared at him.

"What do you mean?"

He could see the bewildered expression on her face and hear the slight tremor in her voice.

"I know you don't trust me and would like nothing more than for me to disappear from your life. But right now, you need to listen to me and do as I ask." His eyes never wavered from hers, imploring her to consider his help, while providing calm strength to her scattered thoughts.

She took a shaky breath and sat back down. "What would you have me do?"

"Everything you need to do can be arranged from here once the police release your apartment."

"Release it?"

"Finish their investigation and allow access. The DEA is working with them since you are part of our case against the Bujazans."

"I see."

"There's more, Brooke."

He spoke in a firm, yet gentle tone, and she found she liked the way her name sounded coming from his lips.

"You have something Paco wants."

Her eyes grew large with confusion.

"It appears Paco may have been passing information to someone at the university using you as the go between. When you were on campus yesterday meeting with Dr. Krueger, a tall, slender male tried to retrieve an object from your leather notebook. One of our agents interrupted him."

Her head began to spin. They'd still been watching her, following her, and she'd had no idea.

"Were you there?"

"Outside. One of my colleagues, the one assigned to watch Paco, followed you into the building. Later, he took pictures of the same man when he met with Paco. We were able to identify him."

"Do you have his name?"

"Perry Worton."

"What?" Brooke could no longer contain her calm at the mention of her ex-fiancé and her eyes blazed with anger.

"Do you know him?"

"I'm surprised his name didn't come up when you did a background check on Brooke," Heath said. "Perry is her ex-fiancé."

"Ex-fiancé, huh? It may be you dodged a major bullet by not marrying Mr. Worton. He's suspected of being an accomplice to the Bujazan drug cartel."

"Perry? That's ridiculous. He wouldn't have the nerve to get involved with any criminal element." His betrayal had been hard, but to think of him breaking the law, and in such a major way, made no sense.

"Do you mind getting your notebook?"

"Not if it will help." Brooke dashed upstairs, anxious to discover what she may have linking her, or rather Paco, to the cartel. She grabbed her notebook, turned it around, looked inside and out, but found nothing to support the agent's theory. "Here you go."

Kade pulled on evidence gloves and took a quick look at the binder before inserting the edge of his knife on one end and splitting the seams, which were held together with an almost imperceptible strip of Velcro. He tapped one end and opened his palm to catch a thin object, the size of a credit card, slipping from the binder. Kade looked up, a smile cracking his normally stoic face.

"What is it?" Annie asked.

"A flash drive." He turned it over to expose the concealed USB connector.

"I've heard they're making them smaller these days, but I've only seen the ones used for business promotions. This one is much slimmer and the connector would be hard to detect." Eric didn't hold out his hand even though he would've liked to inspect it more closely.

"This type is new and can hold up to 16 gigabytes of memory. In a thick binder such as Brooke's, they're virtually undetectable." He looked around the room. "Does anyone have a computer I can use?"

"Follow me." Heath took off toward his office, flipped on the light and fired up his laptop. "Here you go."

Kade slipped the drive into the slot and waited. Within minutes he found himself staring at columns of names, numbers, and dates, as well as code names. He ejected the drive and looked up at Heath.

"It's what I'd hoped to find. Do you have any blank flash drives? I'd like to make some backups."

Heath pulled open a draw and handed Kade three unopened packages.

"They aren't state of the art, but they are 32 gigabytes each."

"This will take a while. Is it all right if I continue to use this?" He tapped the laptop.

"Be my guest. You know where to find us." Heath backed toward the great room, a feeling of déjà vu nagging at him. Something about Kade Taylor triggered a memory. He couldn't place it, didn't know if it were a recent event or one from his past. It hit him the moment he walked into the great room to see Kade looking at the pictures on the wall. He didn't believe it had anything to do with one of the photos. Nevertheless, it tugged at him and wouldn't go away.

"Did he find anything?" Brooke asked as Heath lowered himself next to Annie.

"Yes. He's copying the information to some extra flash drives I had in a drawer."

"So Paco has been using me." Brooke's voice sounded resigned, as if she'd expected it.

Eric knelt down before his sister and took her hands in his.

"It was never about you, Brooke. It appears your fellow student is part of a vicious drug cartel. Hell, his family runs it. He did his job, picking someone without a trace of suspicion around her."

"You mean someone naïve, don't you?"

"No. I mean someone who sees the good in people and trusts them. You're a thousand times better person than Paco is capable of being. He'll be extinguished like

69

the vermin he is. But you? You'll be fine because you are a good person, with strong values, and a pure heart."

Brooke worked to contain the tears forming at her brother's words. Her mind told her he spoke the truth. At the same time, her heart ached knowing she'd been made a fool of, again.

She squeezed Eric's hands. "Thank you." Her voice cracked before she cleared her throat and tried again. "I know you're right. The last week has been hard, now this. I just feel like such a fool."

"This will all work out. I promise. It always does." Eric stood and looked toward his mother and Heath. "I don't know about anyone else, but I'm starving."

They watched him move into the kitchen before Annie spoke up.

"He's right, you know. Perry and Paco are poison, plain and simple. You just got caught in their net." Annie walked over and put her arms around her daughter. "In a few months, we'll be calling you Doctor Sinclair. Your father would be so proud of you."

Kade stood in the hallway, taking in most of the conversation, and feeling a tinge of guilt for his part in the events of the last week. He knew his job depended on his ability to keep suspects at arm's length and work logically through the evidence uncovered. Sometimes all the logic in the world couldn't make up for the destructive outcomes of some of his work. He put a hand over his mouth and coughed, giving them notice of his presence.

"All done, Mr. MacLaren."

Kade grabbed his phone on the second ring. "Taylor."

"Kade, it's Clive. Perry Worton is missing. Took off sometime in the last twelve hours—after the break-in at Miss Sinclair's. He didn't show up for his classes today and his car's gone."

"Any idea where he might have gone?"

"No. My concern is he's on his way to Arizona. Johnson's ordered me to join you. Get me your location and I'll be there later tonight."

"You got it. Thanks, Clive."

Kade turned to see Heath coming up beside him.

"What is it?" Heath asked.

"Looks like you're going to have a couple of visitors— I'll be one of them. Do you have any extra bedrooms?"

"We can work it out. Now, tell me what's happening."

Chapter Five

"Cam, there's been a change in plans. I'm sending you to Montana, along with Doug, and Colt's associate. Jace and I have decided we want to get this evaluation completed sooner than we originally anticipated and either make an offer or tell them no."

Cam and Lainey had stopped by to visit with Brooke and have supper with the family. He'd been surprised to see Agent Taylor, and his mother setting up the guest rooms. Heath's announcement caught him off guard.

"Whatever you want. When are they leaving?"

"Monday on the company plane. Will that work?"

"I'll need to move some appointments, but I can make it work." Cam looked over Heath's shoulder to see Kade talking on his phone. "Excuse me, but what's going on here?"

It didn't take long for Heath to explain what had occurred over the last few hours, culminating in the reaction he'd anticipated.

"I'm not leaving if there's a chance anyone connected to Paco Bujazan will show up here, including Perry Worton."

"Perry only visited here once with Brooke. There's no way of knowing if this is his destination, but Agent Taylor isn't taking any chances. As a precaution, Taylor and his colleague, Clive Nelson, plan to stay at the house. Jace and I will both be here, and I've ordered heightened security around the ranch."

"What about mom, Brooke, and Caroline?"

"They'll stay at Caroline and Jace's place until the situation is resolved."

"And Eric?"

"He'll stay at Jace's with the women. I'm not worried about Lainey as I know she plans to stay in Cold Creek for a week. That's still the case, right?"

Cam shook his head, annoyed he was being shuttled off to Montana while most of the family might be facing danger. "Yes, that's still the plan."

"Good. Make sure she gets out of here." Heath took a swallow of his now cold coffee and set the cup aside. "There's a general alert to law enforcement agencies to watch for Perry. Agent Taylor doubts Perry will ever make it to Fire Mountain."

"And what if Bujazan sends others, or worse, comes himself?"

"It's doubtful he'd put himself in danger. Taylor doesn't believe he has any idea the DEA knew about the transfer or has found the flash drive. For now it appears the most likely person to show up is Perry."

"I hate leaving while all this is going on."

"There's nothing for you to do here. It's important to Jace and me to finalize our review of RTC and make a decision. We don't want to keep Chris and Ty hanging if we don't plan to move ahead."

"And Rafe?"

"To be honest, he's the other reason we want to move fast. Any idea it's MacLaren Cattle looking to buy him out and he'll put up legal roadblocks to kill the deal. Time is our enemy here, Cam."

"Excuse me, Mr. MacLaren. I need to speak with you." Concern showed on Kade's face.

"Whatever you need to say can be said in front of Cam," Heath replied.

"All right. Perry Worton's abandoned car has been found several blocks from his home. We must assume he's rented another one. We're checking with the rental companies and have updated the bulletins sent to all agencies along with his picture."

"And Bujazan?" Cam asked.

"He boarded a private jet headed for Mexico, which isn't surprising. We're going with the theory Mr. Worton is on his way to Fire Mountain to retrieve what he failed to get before." He turned his attention back to Heath. "Our Phoenix office is processing the flash drive now and it appears to be all we hoped."

"Enough to make a case stick?" Heath asked.

"From my perspective, yes. Now it's up to the Assistant D.A, Jeremy Flannigan, and his team. In the meantime, my goal is to keep Worton and anyone else away from you and your family until we can make an arrest." Kade's head swiveled at the sound of Brooke's voice coming from the entry. He spotted her within seconds, noting the smile that made her face light up. He'd love to be the target of one of her smiles sometime.

"Agent Taylor?" Heath said for the second time.

Kade's attention swung back to the other men. "I'm sorry. What did you say?"

Heath would've been amused at the agent's interest in his stepdaughter if they weren't facing such a dangerous situation.

"I asked if there was anything more I could do to support you."

Kade glanced over his shoulder once more, noting Brooke had disappeared down the hall. "Uh...no. I believe we're good for now." He left Heath and Cam staring at his back as he jogged outside, passing Jace and Caroline as they entered the house. A gray, nondescript car made its way up the drive and stopped.

Clive stepped from his car and scanned the area. The main house sat in the middle of a vast amount of acreage. Various types of shrubs and pine surrounded the house, yet didn't produce a dense cover which would make it easy for intruders to hide. He removed his sunglasses to inspect the two story ranch with lots of exterior windows and doors. Although impressive, he knew it would be difficult to protect if anyone did get this far. He doubted that would happen, as so many resources had been deployed to locate and arrest Worton, yet it didn't relieve Kade or him from the responsibility of protecting the family.

"You got here fast." Kade shook Clive's outstretched hand.

"Johnson sent me by air. He's anxious to find a way to wrap this case up."

"We're all anxious to close it. Come inside and I'll introduce you."

Heath, Jace, Cam, and Eric sat around a table, discussing business. Brooke, her mother, and Caroline had just started up the stairs when the agents walked inside.

"Miss Sinclair, I'd like you, your mother, and Caroline to join the rest of us downstairs for a few minutes."

Brooke nodded at Kade, her face devoid of any expression. She'd tried her best to stay clear of him all day, although she'd been less successful than she'd hoped.

"Everyone, this is Special Agent Clive Nelson. He'll be staying here until we know more about what's going on. Clive, this is Brooke's mother, Annie MacLaren, her stepfather, Heath MacLaren, and her brothers, Cam and Eric Sinclair. I believe you know Brooke."

Clive acknowledged each one before turning toward Brooke. "We've haven't been formally introduced, but yes, I do recognize you."

"You're the agent who followed me on campus yesterday, correct?" Brooke asked.

"Yes, I am."

"And you're sure the man who tried to retrieve the information from my binder was Perry Worton? There's no mistake?"

"No, ma'am, no mistake. It's Perry Worton all right. I spoke with him when I interrupted his attempt to recover the flash drive."

"Agent Taylor told us you saw him meet with Paco Bujazan afterwards," Brooke said.

"He showed up at Bujazan's home. I don't believe it's a stretch to connect Perry with the cartel given what I witnessed."

Eric leaned forward in his chair. "He'd be a fool to show up here after what he did to Brooke."

"Perhaps he expects to catch her at the library or somewhere else. She does have a habit of carrying her binder everywhere." Kade's gaze focused on Brooke, and he wondered if she had any idea how much he knew about her habits, and how much more he wanted to learn.

Brooke swung her head to look up at the man who stood just over her shoulder, and felt her breath hitch. He stared directly at her, causing heat to radiate throughout her body, as a jolt of comprehension hit her. She wanted this man, desired him beyond reason. She adjusted her position, trying to quell the unease she felt at the realization she had feelings for Kade, and they weren't disgust or dislike. They were quite the opposite.

"Someone must accompany her everywhere," Annie said.

"I'll drive her wherever she needs to go." Kade's voice was firm and final.

Brooke flashed Kade an irritated glare. She stood and walked around the table to her mother, trying to create as much distance from him as possible.

"Good, that's settled." Clive took a seat next to Cam before continuing. "For now, there's no reason everyone can't go about their business as usual. The ranch is monitored and the house is hard to approach without detection. The one weakness I noticed is the number of windows and doors, which makes it easier for someone to track our movements inside the house. However, I agree with Kade when he says Perry will most likely attempt to intercept Miss Sinclair while she's away from the ranch and has the binder in her possession."

"You noticed the entry to the ranch?" Kade asked Clive.

"I did. The driveway ends about fifty yards from a main intersection. The stores, gas stations, and restaurants will make it easy for someone to park and observe who comes and goes from the property."

"He won't know if she has the binder or not," Heath said.

"Correct. However, we'll assume he'll follow her regardless, believing she'll stick to her normal routine of taking it with her most times." Kade pulled a spiral notepad from his back pocket and made some notes. "Are there any questions?"

"What about notifying local police?" Cam asked.

"Is there someone specific I should speak with?" Clive asked.

"Buck Towers. He's our police chief. I know him pretty well. He was extremely helpful a while back when Lainey was receiving threats when she first moved to Fire Mountain. I can call him if you want."

"No need. We'll handle it," Clive said. "What about your sheriff?"

"Tip Andrews. I have his number." Heath checked his phone and called out the number to Clive.

"Anything else?" Kade waited. He knew the hardest part lay ahead of them. Waiting wasn't easy, even for DEA agents who did it as part of their job. You never got used to the boredom which accompanied sitting around, watching, and trying to stay focused. "All right. Brooke, do you have a few minutes?"

She'd bent down to talk with her mother but shot her gaze up to Kade's when she heard his request. No, I don't have time, she wanted to say. "Of course."

The sun sat tall above Fire Mountain to the west as Kade escorted her outside.

"I hope you don't mind, but I need some air." He reached into another pocket and pulled out one of the electronic cigarettes Brooke had seen others use. "I'm trying to quit. This seems to be the best I can do." He held it up so she could take a look at it.

She'd never seen one this close. "How do you turn it on?" Brooke turned it over in her hand, looking for some type of switch.

Kade took it from her and held it to his mouth then inhaled, letting out a stream of vapor. "Simple." He looked past her to the large barn. "Do you mind if we walk?"

She didn't answer as he started toward a fenced corral. He rested his arms on the top rail and raised a booted foot onto the bottom slat. A couple of horses grazed inside.

"That's my mother's horse, Rascal, and mine, Gremlin. Heath usually keeps Blackjack in his stable unless he's being exercised." She nodded toward the barn.

"Do you ride much?" Kade asked.

"When I'm here, yes, I try to ride every day."

"If there's a horse I can borrow, we can go out if you'd like."

"You ride?" She looked surprised.

He let out a hearty chuckle. "Don't look so surprised." He took another drag from his e-cig while watching the two horses. "I grew up around horses and worked on a ranch during high school. You remember Marshal Salgado? He and I grew up together. His uncle worked for a rancher who hired both of us, full time for four summers and part time during the school year. We learned a lot."

"Did you ever break a horse?"

"Many. And trained the green-broke ones. Sometimes I miss it, but my job keeps me moving around. Between travel and undercover work, I have no time for animals." His voice took on a wistful tone, as if he yearned for more.

"Well then, come on." She grabbed a harness, called Gremlin, led him into the barn, then walked toward a storage area and pulled down her saddle and blanket, throwing them over a rail. "I'll be right back."

Kade watched her leave, picking up the blanket and saddle, and laying them on Gremlin. He'd just finished cinching the saddle in place when Brooke strode inside.

"You have your choice of Blackjack or Rascal."

Kade snorted. "Blackjack."

Brooke watched him approach the magnificent black stallion. She could hear him making soothing sounds, never once flinching when Blackjack sniffed. Others had ridden him, he'd never been trained as a one-man horse, yet it took someone skilled to handle him.

"You're a beauty, aren't you Blackjack," Kade said as he led the horse from his stable and threw the harness rope over a rail.

"This should work for you." Brooke carried a well-worn working saddle, the one Heath preferred.

In no time, the two mounted and started toward the mountains to the west, unaware of the two men watching them from a small patio off Heath's study.

"I can't place him, but I feel as if I've met the man before." Heath continued to watch as they rode out of sight. "Every time we're in the same room I get this prickly sensation. It's eerie."

"It's his walk and mannerisms that caught my attention. Same as you, though, I can't place where I've seen him. Can't say as I know too many DEA agents."

Heath looked at his brother. "How many do you know?"

Jace grinned. "Two. Agent Taylor and Agent Nelson."

******

"How long do you stay when you visit?"

They headed down one of the many rolling hills toward a reservoir in the distance. Kade figured they had about another hour before they needed to start back to the house.

"Usually a few days. Once I finish my degree, I hope to spend a few months here and determine my next steps. I'll be able to work in industry or teach. The truth is, I'm pretty burned out. I've been around a campus environment for so long. I went straight from my undergrad degree to my master's program, then on to the doctorate. I'm ready for a change."

"You're thinking of getting a job in some big corporation?"

"Maybe. Professor Krueger has connected me with two national consulting firms, both looking for people in management systems and operations. That's my field. I'll be meeting with both in the next few months." She shot him a quick glance. "Unless something better comes along."

"You don't sound too excited about it."

Brooke was surprised Kade had picked up on her lack of enthusiasm. She had been wondering for some time why she didn't feel a sense of excitement at her goal being so close, but she just hadn't figured it out yet. She let out a slow breath.

"It's been a long stretch and the last couple of weeks haven't made it any easier. I'd just like to get all this behind me, finish up, defend my dissertation, and come back here."

She'd first thought of making some excuse when he'd told her they needed to talk after the meeting with the family. Now she realized it had been a nervous reaction at the thought of being alone with a man she had such a strong attraction toward. He had an air about him uncommon to most of the men she'd known around campus. If she had to describe him a week ago, she'd have defined Kade Taylor as arrogant, cocky, pushy, and impatient. Her opinion had changed in the last twenty-four hours. She now saw him as confident, comfortable with himself, level-headed, somewhat detached, with a calm demeanor which made others feel secure. She felt safe around him.

"What about you?" Brooke asked as they reined their horses to a stop at the reservoir.

"You mean my job?"

"Yes. Do you see yourself doing this work forever?"

"No, not forever." He'd been struggling with his job in the DEA for several months, needing a change and feeling as if his life had somehow fallen off kilter. He couldn't define the sense of foreboding he'd felt since the last big undercover job almost blew up. Kade looked at Brooke, deciding how much he could say. "A couple of years ago, I'd been given an undercover assignment which lasted much longer than anticipated. It involved a renegade motorcycle gang dealing in drugs and, well, other things."

"Such as?"

"I don't know how much you've read about what some of the gangs are doing, but their activities have stretched well beyond the burglary, assaults, and drug possessions of a few years ago. Some are involved in human trafficking, usually young women and boys, extortion, prostitution rings, money laundering, and associations with Mexican drug cartels."

"Like the Bujazans," Brooke whispered.

"Yes." Kade led Blackjack away from the water and checked his cinch, making a slight adjustment. "There's stuff going on in the clubs most people don't know or care to think about. It's not pleasant, Brooke. But someone has to infiltrate them and try to shut down their operations."

"That's what you were doing?"

He nodded. "In the end, the assignment got out of control, leaving an agent and several gang members dead. We took the main leadership into custody and they're awaiting trial." He thought of the extreme violence he'd witnessed, and become a part of, to achieve his rank in the club. "When it ended, I requested a leave of absence. Bad timing on my part—the department was shorthanded."

Brooke had a long conversation with her mother and Heath earlier while Kade made perimeter checks. Heath encouraged her to understand Kade only did what his job required. They may not like or agree with some of the work men like him had to do, but someone needed to take on tasks no one else wanted to touch, even when they impacted innocent people.

Brooke walked over and placed a hand on Kade's arm. "You were doing your job. What you witnessed and took part in was what you had to do. It's not who you are, Kade. You're a good man, that won't change."

Kade's reaction surprised her. He dropped Blackjack's reins and snaked a hand around her wrist, gently pulling her toward him as his eyes bored into hers. "Is that what you think, Miss Sinclair, that I'm a good man?"

He stared into her wide, crystalline blue eyes, wondering if she felt the same attraction to him as he felt for her. Kade could see her swallow in an attempt to understand his reaction to her comment, her eyes darting to his mouth and back up before her tongue slipped out to moisten her lips.

"Christ," he muttered under his breath, yet didn't let her go.

"I'm sorry. I shouldn't presume to know anything about you, Agent Taylor," she stammered as she tried to step away. He held firm.

Kade searched her face, seeing the same hunger he felt, and the realization rocked him. He closed his eyes, dropped her wrist, and stepped away. No matter their feelings, this wasn't the time or place.

"We'd better start back." He mounted Blackjack and turned toward the ranch.

They rode in silence, Kade trying to make sense of his reaction to her and deriding himself for losing control. Hell, he'd have pulled her into his arms and done what he'd wanted since he'd first seen her on campus if she hadn't tried to pull free. Everything about her made him want what he couldn't have, a normal life.

Brooke did everything possible to control her racing heart. She'd wanted him to draw her closer, against his hard body and kiss her. She'd imagined it all the way from the ranch to the reservoir, and it almost happened. All she would've had to do was take a step closer instead of pulling back. Why had she hesitated?

They rode into the barn, removed the saddles, and brushed down the horses, still saying nothing to each other. Brooke let Gremlin out the back, into the corral with Rascal, while Kade returned Blackjack to his stall.

"I apologize, Miss Sinclair. I never should have touched you."

She closed the back doors and turned toward him. "If you recall, I was the one who reached out to you." She offered a vague smile. "I take full responsibility for your reaction." Brooke laced the halter over a hook. "And, for the record, I didn't mind your reaction one bit."

Chapter Six

Kade glanced over at Brooke from his position by the front window and tried to figure out what she'd meant. He'd been out of line, he knew it. His job was to protect the people in this house from harm, not let his attraction to Brooke hinder his concentration. He needed to protect her while keeping his distance. Even acknowledging it, he still wanted her.

"Anything?" Clive's voice cracked through his ear bud. He'd taken a position outside, closer to a turn leading to the house.

"Nothing here."

"Hold on, I've got a call coming in." He grabbed his phone. "Taylor."

"He's in Fire Mountain," his boss, Dennis Johnson, said. "Used his credit card to check into a motel."

"Thank God for stupid criminals. Give me the details." Kade jotted down the name and address of the hotel. "Do you want us to pick him up?"

"Negative. We want him to get her notebook and try to retrieve the flash drive. Are you set on your end?"

"We are." He'd slipped the original flash drive into her binder earlier in the day, hoping their suspect would make it to Fire Mountain and attempt to locate the data. "I'm taking her into town tomorrow. First stop will be the library where it will be easy for her to leave the notebook unattended."

"Keep me posted."

"Yes, sir." Kade set down his phone and adjusted his ear bud. "Clive, Worton checked into the Valley Motel in Fire Mountain under his own name."

"Isn't the guy some kind of brainiac?" Clive's sarcastic tone came across loud and clear.

"I thought so, but apparently not. Anyway, we're to lure him to the library tomorrow and hope he goes for the binder."

"Roger that. I'm on my way inside."

Kade pulled out the ear bud and shook his head. This was the damnedest case he'd been on in a long time. They were in possession of some of the most damaging material available on the Bujazan drug trade, yet Paco had sent a complete amateur to find and retrieve it. None of it made sense. Unless ...

He strode to the front door as Clive came inside. "Something's not right."

"I agree," Clive responded.

"It's just too easy. The kind of data Paco is passing off is dynamic, it could create massive problems in the cartel operations if it gets out. He'd use his best men on this, right? Instead, he'd got an amateur acting as a courier to locate the missing data. Why would he do that?" Kade asked.

"I've been thinking the same thing." Clive took a seat, leaning forward and letting his arms rest on his knees.

"Remember, Paco is young, spoiled, and arrogant. He's been protected by bodyguards and his father his entire life, and raised to believe he's the golden son who can do no wrong. Given his background, it isn't surprising he believes he's invincible. My guess? It hasn't occurred to him the flash drive is in our possession, or we know he's been using both Miss Sinclair and Mr. Worton as couriers."

"And his father?"

"Paco is doing whatever he can to prove himself to his father. The problem is, he's going about it all wrong. I doubt Francisco Senior is even in the loop on this one."

Clive had spent the last four years following Paco and learning everything he could about the young man. No one knew more about the junior Bujazan than Clive, and nobody wanted him in custody as much as the senior agent.

"You believe we're dealing with a raging case of arrogance?"

"Pretty much."

"Paco's ego is risking an organization worth billions." Kade shook his head. His last assignment, working inside the motorcycle gang, had been nothing like this case. "I wonder what his daddy will do when he learns his son has misplaced such an important package."

"Again, I'm just guessing, but Francisco isn't above making his own son disappear."

"Gentlemen, is there anything we need to know?" Heath walked up beside Kade.

"Perry Worton is in Fire Mountain at the Valley Motel. Do you know it?"

"It's a decent place a mile from the old town area on the highway."

"The plan is to wait until mid-morning before I drive Brooke to the library. I have a hunch Mr. Worton will make his move then and we'll pick him up."

"Seems too easy." Heath crossed his arms and leaned against the door frame.

"We were just discussing the same thing. I guess I'd better let Brooke know." Kade walked toward the sound of her voice coming from the kitchen.

Heath watched him leave, struck again by how familiar the slight swagger seemed. He looked at Clive.

"Where's Taylor from?"

"You mean originally? Wyoming or Montana. I can't remember which."

Heath pushed from the wall and followed Kade into the kitchen, hearing his deep voice explaining the plan for tomorrow to Brooke. He walked into the room in time to see Brooke rest her hand on his arm and Kade lean slightly toward her. Annie had been right. Something was definitely going on between the DEA agent and his stepdaughter.

Brooke dropped her hand as Heath approached and stepped toward the counter.

"Kade's been explaining what I need to do tomorrow."

"Are you okay with it? If you're uncomfortable, I'm certain Agent Taylor can work out another plan. Right?" Heath's gaze locked on Kade.

"I'm fine with the plan. There's no need to change anything. Believe me, I want them to nail Perry and I want to be there when they do it."

"Ah, a little vengeance?" Kade asked.

"Of course not. Well, maybe a little." Color crept up Brooke's neck. "I know it sounds awful, but..." Her voice trailed off. She didn't know how much Kade knew about her breakup with Perry, preferring he knew as little as possible.

"Hey, the guy's a jerk and most likely a criminal. No need to feel bad at all about wanting him arrested." Kade grabbed a couple of cookies from the counter then turned to lean against it. "Wow, these are great. Your wife make them?"

"Annie loves to bake when she's nervous and this whole situation has her tense. We may end up with enough to open a bakery by the time this is all over. Well, time I turned in. See you two in the morning."

Brooke placed a kiss on his cheek. "I'm not far behind you."

"Goodnight, Mr. MacLaren." Kade finished off the second cookie and wiped his hands on his slacks. "Clive and I will take turns watching out the front."

"I thought you believed the chances of anyone coming here were slim."

"They are, but it pays to be cautious. I'll see you tomorrow, Brooke."

******

"And Cam, I'd like to speak with you again tonight about your first impressions of RTC." Heath hung up the phone as Kade entered the study. "Good morning, Taylor."

"Mr. MacLaren. You're up early."

Heath checked the time. Eight o'clock. "I'm at my desk here at home by six at the latest, then I usually drive to the office. Today, I'll stay here, for obvious reasons. Can I do anything for you?"

"I wanted to let you know the call you made to Buck Towers paid off. He just called. They set up surveillance at the motel. Worton stayed inside all night, but took off a little while ago. He's driving toward the ranch and there's a problem. He has someone else with him—a beefy looking Hispanic man. The deputy took a photo and is trying to get an identification, but odds are, he's one of Paco's men."

"Does his presence change your plans?" Heath asked.

"That's what I want to talk with you about. Clive will follow us to town and stay outside to keep an eye on Worton's companion. Chief Towers will also have men posted outside the library. I can call Towers or the sheriff to see if they can send some men out here to keep watch while we're gone."

"No. I've got my own people. You don't have any indication there are more of Bujazan's men around, right?" Heath asked.

"No, sir. It appears to be just Worton and whoever is with him."

"We'll be fine then."

"All right. I'll go check with Clive." Kade started to leave before turning at Heath's words.

"Taylor, one more thing. You'd better keep a good watch on Brooke. Anything happens to her and I'll hold you personally responsible. Are we clear?"

"Yes, sir. Quite clear."

******

"Are you ready?" Kade asked as he and Brooke walked toward her car.

She shaded her eyes and glanced up at him. "Yes. Let's get this over with."

They'd decided she'd drive while Kade stayed out of sight in the back, figuring Perry would be able to recognize her car. Clive left earlier to park next to one of the restaurants where he'd have a good view of the ranch entrance as well as anyone following Brooke's car. Thanks to Buck Towers, they had the description of Perry's car. Clive had already confirmed the car was in the lot with both Mr. Worton and his friend inside. As they all hoped, Perry took the bait and pulled onto the highway a few cars behind Brooke.

Kade checked the time. If everything went as planned, Perry Worton would be in jail within a few hours, telling them everything he knew about Paco Bujazan.

Brooke parked outside the library, grabbed the notebook, and glanced in the back seat.

"Don't take any chances. Find a spot, work a while, then leave the binder while you walk around the bookshelves. Stay away long enough for Perry to snatch it and leave. The rest of it will be up to us."

Brooke didn't reply, just took one long look at Kade, and closed the car door. She spotted Clive's car right away as well as one of Buck Towers' men talking to another gentleman at the second entrance. She sucked in a deep breath and walked inside.

"There she is." Perry spotted Brooke from his parked car and glanced at Julio, whose large frame appeared jammed into the seat of the small sedan. He'd be glad to get rid of the bodyguard and back to his normal life. All he needed to do was retrieve the flash drive, pass it on to the professor in the biotechnology department at the university, and he'd be done. From there it would be transferred to the last recipient. Perry had no idea what they would do with the drive or even what information it contained. All he knew was this would be his last job for Paco Bujazan. "Wonderful. She has the binder." He pushed the door open but stopped when he felt Julio's strong grip on his arm.

"Do not fail again. I will be watching you from inside." Julio's feral glare and chilling message cut through Perry, who broke into a cold sweat.

It didn't take long for Perry to find Brooke seated at one of the work stations. He watched as she opened her binder, then pulled a spiral notepad from her purse and began to write. All he had to do was wait for the opportunity to grab that flash drive. He picked up a magazine and sat in a large upholstered chair far enough away she wouldn't see him, with an excellent view if she walked away. He didn't wait long.

Brooke heard the tone indicating she'd received a text message. She knew it must be from Kade, telling her Perry had entered the library. She checked it anyway, then tried to look around without being obvious. Clive lounged against a pillar with a book in hand. He nodded to his left, indicating Perry's location. She stood, grabbed her purse, and looked for the ladies room.

Perry stayed seated until Brooke disappeared around a corner. He dropped the magazine and wandered toward the desk, looked around, and sat down, pulling the binder toward him. He slipped a finger between two seams, popped the nylon strips, and let the drive slip into his hand. Pocketing it, Perry set the binder back on the desk, stood, and turned right into the path of Clive and a uniformed policeman.

"Perry Worton, you're under arrest ..."

That was all Perry heard before fainting into the arms of the surprised agent.

******

Julio hid behind a long row of books and watched as Worton regained consciousness, was cuffed, and led outside. He dashed out of the library, planning to reach the car and drive off before anyone saw him. Julio slipped behind the wheel, inserted the key, and froze at the sound of tapping on his window. He dropped a hand, trying to reach between the seats where he'd hidden a gun.

"I wouldn't." Kade's command rang through the glass and Julio turned to see the wrong end of a Sig Sauer staring him in the face. "Put your hands back on the steering wheel."

Julio complied as Kade pulled open the door and motioned for him to get out. He glanced around to see two other uniformed officers pointing similar weapons at him and realized there would be no escape.

"Kade, one of the officers will take Miss Sinclair home. The other deputies will help us escort the prisoners to jail." Clive touched Perry on the back, motioning for him to start walking as the other policemen kept their guns trained on Julio.

"Give me a minute." Kade dashed toward Brooke who stood next to her car, watching the scene. He could see the color drain from her face and she grabbed at the car door for balance as his arm wrapped around her.

"It's all right, Brooke. It's over. We have Perry and it's all because of you. You did great."

She leaned into him and let her head rest on his shoulder, taking the comfort he offered. Kade was right. She could see Perry being marched toward the jail a block away and the other man being handcuffed by two officers. The ordeal had ended and no one had been hurt.

He could feel her breathing even out and she pulled back.

"Thank you," she whispered before slipping into her car and resting her head against the seat.

Kade watched as the officer pulled away, taking her home to her family.

"Kade, you coming?" Clive asked as he started across the street with Perry in tow.

"Yeah, I'm coming." He took once last look at the red SUV driving away and decided he needed to find a way to stay in Fire Mountain for a little while longer.

******

"Julio Menendez is what his identification says." Clive spoke into his phone, relaying the arrest details to Dennis Johnson back in San Diego. "Kade and I will be questioning Perry first, then turn our attention to his partner. Yes, sir, I will."

"You know we don't have much on Menendez." Kade leaned against a wall as he scanned the questions he had for Worton.

"We can make him sweat for a while."

"You know he won't talk. He'll wait until Paco sends an attorney."

"If he sends one. Julio might just be expendable. Well, let's get started with Worton." Clive opened the door to the interrogation room and followed Kade inside.

Perry sat erect, his hands shaking even though he clasped them tight, causing the knuckles to turn white. Perspiration beaded on his forehead and he looked as though he'd be sick at any minute.

"Can I get you some coffee or water, Mr. Worton?" Kade asked from his position across the table.

"No, nothing."

"In case you've forgotten, I'm Special Agent Nelson and this is Special Agent Taylor. We're both with the DEA."

Perry glared at them, throat working. "I remember."

"Why don't you tell us what happened in the library and why you were in possession of a flash drive containing data directly related to the Bujazan drug cartel?"

******

Brooke's head ached by the time the officer pulled to a stop in front of the MacLaren house. The headaches from her concussion had lessened each day, and she'd thought they were behind her, but the stress of today had ignited a doozy. She longed for a hot compress and a soft pillow.

"How did it go?" Annie asked as she wrapped an arm around Brooke.

"They were right. Perry came after the flash drive and now he's in custody. Kade and Clive are questioning him. It's over."

Annie pulled away, noticing the grimace on Brooke's face and suspecting she'd reached her limit. "How's your head?"

"About to explode." She tried to make light of it but failed. "I'm going upstairs for a while."

She kicked off her sandals, slipped out of her jeans, and crawled under the covers, already beginning to feel better. Although she'd been around guns her whole life, she'd still had an anxious moment watching Kade in action. He'd surprised her by walking up and wrapping an arm around her, quashing the unexpected shaky feeling which ripped through her body. The feel of him pulling her close triggered much more than just a sense of comfort.

She knew he'd return to the ranch, if for no other reason than to pick up his truck. He'd come to Fire Mountain for a purpose, to obtain the data and arrest whomever came after it. Kade's job would now take him back to San Diego, or wherever the agency sent him next. Brooke wondered if she'd ever see him again after today and felt a sharp stabbing sensation in her chest. She wasn't ready to let him out of her life, yet she had no way of holding him. Her head reminded Brooke the strong attraction had everything to do with lust and nothing more. Her heart told her otherwise.

Her eyes closed as she remembered their ride to the reservoir. She'd learned so much about him, yet she was certain there were secret depths to Kade Taylor that had yet to be revealed. She wanted to know them all.

"Brooke, are you asleep?"

Brooke woke from a deep sleep and stretched. "No, I'm awake."

Annie walked in and smiled at her daughter who still lay cocooned in her bed. "How's your headache?"

"Gone for now." She threw back the covers and swung her feet to the floor, before noticing the sun no longer shone through her bedroom window. "What time is it?"

"After seven. Agents Taylor and Nelson have been in with Heath for over an hour. Every once in a while I hear them laughing, then all goes quiet."

"Do you know what happened with Perry?"

"Just that they are waiting for a couple of U.S. Marshals to arrive to escort Perry and the other man to San Diego. It's doubtful they'll arrive before tomorrow." Annie strode toward the hallway and turned back. "I thought you'd like to know, in case you have questions."

Brooke grabbed her jeans and top, then ran into the bathroom. Five minutes later, she'd dressed and took the stairs at a fast pace. She told herself her interest lay in the need to know about Perry and whether or not he confessed. In truth she wanted, no, she needed, to see Kade. She stopped at the study door and knocked.

"Come in." Heath saw Brooke poke her head inside and motioned for her to take a seat.

"I'm not interrupting anything, am I?" Brooke's heart tripped over itself at the way Kade allowed his gaze to sweep over her in frank appraisal. "You have news?"

"He sang like a bird." Kade let his eyes roam over her tight jeans, clingy white t-shirt, and slim sandals. She'd pulled her blond hair into a ponytail and wore no makeup. He had to control the intense desire which swept through him at the sight.

"That's great news." Her voice sounded breathless and husky at his unguarded assessment of her. "Mother told me a couple of marshals are coming to town to escort the men to San Diego." She took a seat on a leather sofa, folding her hands in an attempt to still the sensations which wouldn't be stilled.

"Mr. Worton, yes. Unfortunately, we can't hold Julio Menendez much longer with what we have."

"But, I thought..." her voice trailed off.

Kade stood and walked to the sofa, taking a seat next to Brooke. "There's no reason to believe Paco will send more men to come after you or your family. He's back in Mexico with his family and the damage is already done. They wanted the flash drive, nothing more."

Brooke squirmed and tried to edge away at the sense of heat radiating from Kade's body. She ran a hand around the neck of her t-shirt then brushed a hand across her forehead.

"Are you all right?" Kade cast her a somber yet knowing look, as if he, too, felt the same sensations.

"Yes, fine," she said, and cleared her throat. "Well, I guess you and Agent Nelson will be heading back to San Diego." Brooke stood and took a few steps to the edge of the desk, leaning a hip against it.

"As soon as the marshals take Worton into custody." Kade's eyes searched her face for any trace of regret at his imminent departure, but she kept her features hooded. He stood and walked toward the door. "I'd better get the paperwork finished."

"Will you join us for dinner?" Heath asked.

Kade took one more quick glance at Brooke before responding, noticing her expression still hadn't changed. "That would be great."

Chapter Seven

Brooke lounged in the big upholstered chair she used for reading and tried to concentrate. The study had become her safe haven, a place she went to be alone and think. Tonight the peace she sought escaped her.

Eric had stopped by in time for dinner and now gathered with the other men in the great room. She could hear their voices and laughter as each contributed stories to the conversation. They'd asked her to join them, but she'd declined, preferring to start the process of distancing herself from the man she most wanted to be around. Brooke had been down this path before, with Perry, falling for someone who had no intention of ever staying faithful. She didn't see Kade as the same type of man—the differences between them were great. However, a job which created a nomadic lifestyle for the DEA agent, coupled with her insecurities about relationships, made it difficult to contemplate any type of relationship between the two of them.

"Am I interrupting you?"

Brooke looked up at the sound of the familiar voice and closed the book. Her gaze moved upward and locked on Kade's deep green eyes. She wondered if he had any idea how she felt about him.

"Not at all."

"Your mother is serving dessert and coffee. I thought I'd take a walk afterwards. Would you come with me?"

Say yes, she told herself. "I'm pretty beat. Can I take a rain check?"

His mouthed curved upward. They both knew the likelihood of seeing each other after tonight were slim. "Sure, Brooke." He pulled a card from his pocket and held it out to her. "In case you threw away the first one I gave you."

She took the card, knowing she wouldn't use it. If he wanted to see her again, he'd have to be the one to make the first move once they were both back in San Diego.

"How about dessert, you two?" Annie poked her head in the library and held up the tray in her hand. "Come up for air, Brooke. It's one of your favorites."

She followed Annie into the dining room, Kade right behind her, and took her usual seat. This time he grabbed the chair next to her, brushing her thigh with his as he sat down. She tried to scoot her chair over, only to find she'd been wedged between Eric on one side and Kade on the other.

"Any word from Cam?" Eric asked Heath as he scooped some cobbler into a large bowl.

"He spent the day going over the buy out details with all three partners. So far, he's impressed with the operation and hopes to wrap everything up within the week." Heath sipped his coffee and shot a look at Jace. He and his wife Caroline had stopped by to learn the outcome of the day's events and talk about the proposed acquisition. Heath and Jace both knew if they decided to proceed, they'd be facing a major obstacle in Rafe. Neither looked forward to the inevitable confrontation.

"Will either of you be heading up there?" Annie asked. She knew the difficulties with the purchase. In her heart, she hoped it would go through and perhaps reunite the three brothers.

Heath glanced at Kade and Clive, hesitant to say too much in front of them. Both knew MacLaren Cattle had been looking to buy a company in Montana. The business and partner names hadn't been shared.

"It's doubtful. We believe the deal may have a better chance if Cam is the lead negotiator."

"Do you go through this often, purchasing other companies?" Kade asked, taking the opportunity to shift in his chair and lean a shoulder against Brooke's at the same time his leg found a comfortable spot resting against hers.

"Lately, it seems we're doing more of it than anything else," Jace said as he finished off his cobbler. "All the businesses are connected, so we're expanding where we already have expertise."

Kade looked at Brooke. "Once you finish your degree, will you be applying your skills to the family business?"

Brooke choked and grabbed for a water glass at the same time Kade patted her a couple of times on the back.

"Are you all right?"

"Fine." She coughed again and noticed Kade had yet to move his hand from her back. Instead, he rubbed slow circles with his palm. The contact sent shivers through her body and heat spiraling up her neck and face, before he let his hand drop to rest on his thigh.

"We've never spoken with Brooke about a role at MacLaren, although Jace and I have discussed the possibility on numerous occasions."

"You have?" she asked, surprised they'd even consider her experience as benefiting the company.

"Of course. We're expanding and your knowledge of management systems could prove valuable in tying the businesses together."

The room quieted as Brooke absorbed this new turn of events.

"All right, time for me to take off." Eric grabbed his empty plate and started for the kitchen.

The others followed, with Caroline and Brooke helping Annie clean up after shooing the men from the kitchen. The women needed their own time and this seemed to be the most suitable place.

"What's with you and Kade?" Caroline asked as she rinsed and placed silverware in the dishwasher.

"I don't know what you mean." Kade wasn't someone Brooke wanted to discuss, especially when her feelings for him were so new.

"Come on, Brooke. He couldn't keep his eyes off you."

"Or his hand when you had the coughing spell," Annie added.

"Come on, Mom. Can you imagine someone like Kade being interested in a woman like me? Boring, bookworm,

Brooke. He'd go for excitement and someone, well, you know." She illustrated with her hands the type of women she thought Kade would find attractive. "We're as different as any two people could be."

"You don't believe two people who are opposites can find happiness?" Caroline asked.

"I didn't say that. Look, he rides a chopper, and works undercover in some of the worst motorcycle and drug gangs around. Do you know what members in those clubs have to do to be accepted?"

Both Annie and Caroline stopped what they were doing. "What?"

"He wasn't specific, but I checked several of the clubs on the Internet and what they do is graphic and public. Kade lives on the edge, while I live comfortably within the walls of a large university." She took a breath, wishing it were otherwise.

"If he did ask to see you, what would you say?" Annie asked.

She let out a slow breath. "Honestly, I don't know. The smart choice would be to tell him no, for all the reasons I mentioned." She leaned against a counter and folded the towel in her hand. "The problem is, I can't think straight when he's around."

Annie and Caroline shot a quick look at each other. Both had gone through the same mental confusion when dating their husbands, Heath and Jace.

"And if he wants to be friends?"

"That's a good question. He's a complicated man who tends to keep his personal life to himself. Truthfully, I don't know much about him, except I believe he has a good heart, is dedicated to his job, and works hard."

"Is it possible you'd ever run into him once you get back to school?" Caroline asked.

"It's doubtful. His world and mine are just too different."

Brooke fell silent. She couldn't afford to get involved with someone whose life centered on adrenaline pumping, on-the-edge assignments. When she met the right man, he'd be more like her, with a love for books and academics. Perhaps one of the professors on campus or a corporate type, the kind of men who visited the school in search of new ideas. Three-piece-suit men with a list of credentials behind their names. A leather-clad, motorcycle riding, action-centered drug agent would never find someone like her appealing. The type of life she led, aside from the last few weeks, would bore Kade before long and he'd end up seeking someone more exciting, breaking her heart in the process.

This time she'd use her head. She'd meet someone using logic and care, tactics she understood and could control. No more jumping into a relationship and getting her insides twisted up when it didn't work out.

******

"I'm heading to bed. Will we see you in the morning?" Clive directed his question to Heath.

"Count on it."

"I think I'll head outside. You mind if I check on the horses?" Kade asked.

"Be my guest, just don't get too attached. Blackjack's my horse," Heath joked as Kade disappeared out the front door.

He strode to the barn, pulling out his e-cig and inhaling, blowing the vapor out into the warm night air. He'd hoped Brooke would join him, share more about herself, and her plans. His attraction to the girl-next-door, Ph.D. candidate made no sense, yet it slammed into him whenever she was anywhere around. Kade had always gone for women rough around the edges, who understood his lifestyle, and didn't form attachments. Most had made it through life the hard way, as he had, without the aid of a rich family or social connections. He liked women who could relate to his need for excitement and danger. A sophisticated woman such as Brooke would never find a man like him anything more than a passing interest. She moved in circles he'd never feel comfortable in, and expect a life he couldn't provide.

He inhaled again and walked toward Blackjack's stall. No other word could be used for him except magnificent. The sleek black coat and lines took Kade's breath away every time he saw the stallion. Someday he'd own an animal such as this.

"I thought you might still be in here."

The soft, almost tentative voice caught him by surprise. He spun toward her and stared. She'd changed into tight fitting black jeans and a sleeveless peach colored top which draped in front. He let his eyes wander over every curve, not caring if she noticed. Her hair cascaded down her shoulders and shown in the bright moonlit night. He took several long strides toward her, stopping a few feet away.

Brooke rested her back against the wall of the barn and wiped her damp hands on her jeans. The decision to change and meet him had been impulsive, completely at odds with what she'd told her mother and Caroline just an hour before. Her need to see him, talk with him once more before he left had overpowered her common sense, making a lie of all her earlier resolutions.

"Why did you come?"

She closed her eyes, not sure her answer would make any sense. "I'm not quite certain. To say thank you, and goodbye. Our lives are so different...the chances so small we'll ever see each other again. I didn't want you to leave without knowing how much you being here has meant to me." Her heart hammered in an almost painful rhythm and she worked to draw a breath. She let her eyes drop to his chest, then move up to his mouth which had curved into a wry smile.

Kade took a step closer, his gaze boring into hers, his face a mask.

"You're right, you know." His voice held no inflection, leaving her to wonder if he felt anything for her.

Her brows drew together. "About what?"

"You and I, we're worlds apart." He reached out, drawing his knuckles down her cheek and over her jaw before letting his hand drop to his side. "I won't lie to you, Brooke. I want you, more than I've ever wanted a woman. But wanting you isn't enough. You deserve someone with roots, without the memories and baggage I carry." His lips curved into a self-deprecating smirk as he opened his arms and looked toward his scuffed boots and torn jeans. "Look at me, Brooke. Your future is with a man who can match your brains and style, not someone who has no home and slums with drug dealers and killers."

She listened in her usual calm manner, letting him get it all out, and looking at the picture he made standing before her. He had no idea how much she wanted him and how much it hurt to acknowledge he'd told the truth. She couldn't let herself be controlled by her desires. The man she'd build a life with would have roots, be there at night, share life's burdens, and be more interested in their kid's upcoming soccer game than in the next arrest.

"It's funny. I came in here determined not to let you know how much your leaving hurts. Now I must confront it." She walked toward one of the stalls and grabbed a lead line, took one end and began to twirl in a circle. "You know, Kade, I've been fortunate. My father was a man of strong values. He had principles which never wavered. In that, he and my stepfather are much alike. Do you know what one of their firm beliefs is?" She kept her voice calm as she strolled to him, twirling the rope in front of her.

"No, what?" Kade watched her, captivated by her image.

"Tell the truth. No matter what, don't cough up a lot of bull because you can't handle delivering what needs to be said."

"Is that what you think I did? Hand you a load of bull?" His voice took on an ominous tone as his eyes narrowed at her implication he'd lied.

"No, it's what I'd been prepared to hand you." She turned and tossed the lead line over the top of a stall and looked back at Kade. "You had the courage to confront it. I didn't." She took a breath and walked to within a foot of him. "The attraction I have toward you is so strong some nights, I can't sleep. Each time you're around, my heart races and I can hardly think or breathe. Like you, I tell myself over and over it would never work. I need a life you could never give me, and you need someone who lives on the edge, not within the safe walls of a home or university." She looked to the ground and closed her eyes, trying to speak her last thoughts before gazing back up at him. "You have no idea how much I wish I were a different person and could be what you want."

Kade swallowed the lump in his throat and moved to within inches of her, lifting her chin with a finger and staring into her beautiful eyes.

"If only," he said and brushed her lips with his before pulling her into his arms, and covering her mouth in a raw, sensual kiss which had her senses reeling. It wasn't a gentle kiss, but demanding and passionate—everything Brooke had imagined it would be.

She wrapped her arms around his neck and pulled tight, feeling the queue at the back of his neck. She tugged on the leather thong, letting his hair fall loose, and running her fingers through the loose strands.

Kade's hands moved up and down her back, molding her to him, and feeling her softness against his muscled body. He felt his control slip further and knew this had to stop. What he'd told her before had been the truth, at least the part he'd been willing to divulge. The rest she'd never learn—not from him. No matter how each felt, there would be no future for them. He gentled the kiss, drew back on a ragged breath, and rested his forehead against hers.

"Ah, Brooke, how I wish it could be different." He placed one more kiss on her lips before heading toward the house, not once looking back over his shoulder.

******

Brooke knew her actions branded her a coward. She glanced at her clock. Six in the morning. She could hear Kade talking with Heath and her mother outside as he prepared to leave to meet the marshals at the jail. She assumed he'd be following them back to San Diego. After last night, Brooke knew seeing him again wouldn't accomplish anything.

She threw back the covers and plodded to the window, pulling open the shutters enough to see him standing with the truck door open. He glanced up, toward her room, before climbing inside and slamming the door. She stayed planted by the window, watching as he drove down the long driveway and out of sight.

"Brooke, you up?"

"Yes, Mom. Come on in."

"You didn't come down to see Agent Taylor off."

"I just woke up, and well, you and Heath were with him. It seemed pointless for me to dress and rush downstairs to repeat what I said last night." She pulled her hair into a ponytail then straightened up her bed, hoping her mother wouldn't notice how dejected she felt. From past experience, she knew the feeling would last two, maybe three days, then she'd start the process of forgetting. In the meantime, she'd concentrate on preparing to defend her dissertation when she returned to campus in another week.

"I'm getting breakfast ready, so come down as soon as you're done here." Annie took one last glance at Brooke then shut the door. She knew something still troubled her daughter and didn't believe it had to do with finalizing her doctoral program. With Perry in custody, there could be just one reason for Brooke's blue mood, and he'd driven away minutes before.

******

114

"One more signature and you can get out of here." The deputy collected the forms and called to someone behind her to take U.S. Marshal Ernesto Salgado and Special Agent Taylor to the back of the station where Nesto and another marshal would accompany Perry Worton to a waiting van.

"I understand you spent the last few days at Miss Sinclair's ranch." Nesto leaned against a wall as they prepared the prisoner for the transfer.

"Her parents' ranch." Kade stood a couple of feet away, not the least bit interested in discussing Brooke or her family.

"And?"

"And what?"

"Hey, man, you know what I'm asking. You couldn't take your eyes off Miss Sinclair when we brought her in for questioning. Are you telling me you didn't make a move after you found out she had nothing to do with Paco?"

"It wasn't like that."

"You forget who you're speaking to. I would've placed money on you already—"

"Enough, Nesto."

Salgado's eyes narrowed as he focused more closely on his friend of well over fifteen years. "So it's like that, is it?"

"Leave it alone." Kade locked eyes with Nesto, his gaze indicating the conversation had ended.

Nesto walked up and clasped Kade's shoulder. "Sorry, man," Nesto said, and meant it. He'd never seen a woman get to his friend like this—one he couldn't walk away from.

"Here you are, gentlemen." A young deputy came to a stop, Peter Worton beside him.

"Thanks. We'll take it from here." Salgado took the prisoner by his elbow and escorted him outside where the other marshal waited. It didn't take long to secure Worton in the back of the van and lock the doors. "Are you following us?" he asked Kade, who stood watch, not trusting Paco wouldn't try to break free, or kill any man who could put him in prison.

"Might as well."

Nesto climbed inside and leaned out the window. "Drinks tonight at Water's Edge."

Kade waved as he walked to his truck. Might as well get drunk, nothing else sounded good, and he certainly couldn't have what he wanted.

Chapter Eight

"I can't find anything wrong with RTC, Heath. It's as clean as the Colorado purchase." Cam held the phone between his shoulder and ear, looking over some notes as he scribbled in a journal. "There's nothing else to check and they've answered all my questions. How do you want to proceed?

"Come on back. I'll set up a meeting with Jace, Eric, Doug, and Colt so we can plan our next steps." Heath hung up the phone and punched another number. "Ask Jace to stop by my office when he has a chance."

Half of him had hoped Cam would find a deal killer. The other half accepted the issue he and Jace would face if they made an offer.

Heath grabbed a bottle of water, unscrewed the cap and gulped it down. What he wanted filled a brown bottle in a closed cupboard a few feet away, but it would have to wait.

"You wanted to see me?" Jace strolled in and pulled back a chair.

"I heard from Cam."

"And?"

"The deal makes sense."

Jace took a minute to let the news sink in. They weren't the type of men who walked away from good business opportunities. This might have to be the first.

"Pros and cons?" Jace asked.

"Hell, there are too many pros to list and only one con."

"Rafe. He's a big issue, Heath, not some insignificant glitch in the deal."

"True." He picked up his latest notes from Cam and slid them across the desk to Jace. "If the price is right, we'd be fools to leave RTC for someone else to scoop up."

Jace read through the information, asked a few questions, then set the paper down.

"What are you thinking?"

Heath jotted down a number on his notepad and turned it toward Jace.

"Seems reasonable. Start lower and work up to this if necessary."

"We'll go through the details when Cam gets back in town. My thought is to have him handle the negotiations as long as possible." Heath settled into his chair and leaned back.

Jace made no move to leave. "It shouldn't be happening like this, with Rafe on the outside. I hate doing this to him."

"We both do. We have two choices—go after the company or walk away. I'll be okay with either."

"The hell you will. You've never backed off a good business deal in your life, and this is a great one."

"This may be the first time." Heath's voice held none of the firm confidence everyone associated with him.

Jace slapped his palms on Heath's desk and stood. "Call the meeting. We'll study the details and make a decision like any other purchase, taking Rafe out of the picture. We'll focus on the numbers, like we always do, and make a business decision."

Heath watched as Jace closed the door and thought of the last time they'd seen Rafe.

The three brothers and their father, Clark MacLaren, had been discussing expanding the horse breeding business. Rafe wanted to move into a new and expanding area, providing stock for rodeos, both broncs and bucking bulls. He believed opportunities existed in both, especially the bull market. Heath and Jace thought both might be ideas to consider in the future. However, right then, neither could throw their support to Rafe.

Their father wanted no part of the expansion—at that time or in the future, calling it a fool's venture. Rafe's face had turned to stone.

"And if one of your real sons had brought it up, would it hold more value?" Rafe asked in a cold, calm voice.

His question hit their father like a punch to the gut. He pushed up from the massive oak and leather chair, glaring at his middle boy.

"You are my son, same as Heath and Jace," Clark ground out.

"No, not the same. You'll never see me as anything more than the mistake you made years ago. I'll never hold the same place in this family and all of you know it." Rafe grabbed his hat. "I'm done." He'd stormed out the door, hooked up his trailer to the old Chevy truck he'd purchased doing odd jobs, loaded the two horses he'd earned through hard work and sweat, and drove away.

They all thought he'd blow off his anger and return. They'd been wrong. Clark died a few years later, knowing his middle son had ended up in Montana. Stubborn pride had kept their father from reaching out and trying to mend the rift. Nevertheless, he'd split his estate evenly between the three, designating Heath to take on the role of president of the MacLaren businesses.

The sound of his phone ringing pulled Heath from the painful memory and back to the present.

"Give me thirty minutes and I'll be there." He hung up, glad Annie had reminded him of Brooke's plan to leave for San Diego that afternoon. He'd take his wife and stepdaughter to lunch, and give himself a respite from thinking about old feuds and future conflicts.

******

Brooke hit the interstate doing seventy-five. Her windows were open and the radio blasted a mix of country songs. She'd preferred jazz before her mother had married into the MacLaren family. Now she switched between the two and enjoyed all of it.

The last two weeks had gone from a crawl to flying by with little time to think of Kade Taylor. The first few days were rough, remembering the night before he left and wishing she'd had the courage to follow her heart and not her head. She told herself the outcome would've been the same either way. He had no stomach for a woman like her, but the thought didn't help ease the pain.

Brooke had been given a date to appear before her program committee to defend her dissertation. Three weeks ago, she'd felt the need for more time to prepare. Now, she wanted to get these final steps behind her and move on.

Heath and Jace had met with her twice to discuss ways her education and experience could benefit the MacLaren companies. The compensation sounded more than fair, she'd have her own place, similar to Eric's two bedroom cabin, and lots of freedom to design management integration systems. It sounded perfect. Why wasn't she more excited?

The sun had set and she felt bone tired by the time she pulled into her spot at the tiny apartment complex. With the help of her neighbor, she'd taken care of the insurance, getting the apartment cleaned and repaired, and installing new locks while she stayed in Fire Mountain. God bless her neighbor. She owed the elderly woman several dinners and maybe a trip to the movies. The woman did love her action flicks.

Brooke rolled her bag into the living room and kicked the door closed. Everything seemed the same except for missing vases and picture frames which Perry had destroyed in his attempt to locate the flash drive. She kicked off her sandals and fell onto the couch, thinking of

Kade, wondering if she'd ever run into him again, and if he ever thought of her.

An image of him laughing at a comment Clive made crossed her mind. He had the sexiest smile of any man she'd ever known—she wished he'd flashed it more often. She closed her eyes and let the memory of the night they'd said goodbye wash over her. If only things were different, she thought, right before exhaustion claimed her.

******

"Yes, I have it, sir. I'll be there in thirty." Kade shoved the phone back in his pocket. He'd parked outside Brooke's apartment building, where he'd been ever since Clive told him Brooke left Arizona for San Diego.

Kade watched Brooke enter her apartment, considering if it was wise or foolish to knock on her door. Foolish won out and he stayed seated on his chopper, doo rag around his head, and helmet resting in his lap. He thought of his last night at the ranch. She'd made a comment which played over and over in his mind the last few weeks.

You have no idea how much I wish I were a different person and could be what you want.

He'd let it go, not correcting her belief she wasn't what he wanted. It would be better for her to think that than to know the truth. He wanted no other woman—only Brooke Sinclair.

Kade slid the helmet on his head, took one more look at her apartment, and rode off. In a matter of hours, he'd be free to do anything for the next ninety days. Anything except what he most wanted.

******

Kade tossed the paperwork on his kitchen table before grabbing a cold beer. He had to make a decision, and quick. His lease expired at the end of the month. Its location near the water and the manageable rent made up for the fact the place was a dump. Leaky faucets, faulty appliances, and a sieve for a roof didn't bother Kade as much as committing to another six months.

Salgado purchased a two bedroom, two bath place with a harbor view several months ago. His situation didn't compare to Kade's. Nesto knew he'd be based in San Diego for a long time, whereas Kade didn't know the location of his next assignment until weeks or sometimes just days beforehand. Nesto had told Kade he'd always have a place to crash and to not worry about renting an apartment. Maybe his friend was right.

Kade reached for another beer and twisted off the cap, flipping it into an open trash can a few feet away as his phone rang.

"Taylor."

"Agent Taylor, this is Heath MacLaren."

Kade sat up and set his beer down. "Yes, sir. What can I do for you?"

"I have a proposition for you, if you have a few minutes to talk."

"As long as you need."

"Brooke indicated you're up for a leave of absence. Is that true?"

The question came from out of nowhere. "Yes. In fact I received approval today. My leave starts tomorrow."

"Made any plans?" Heath asked.

"No, sir, not yet. Truth is, I'm not sure what I'll do with the time." Kade settled a hand around the beer bottle, rotating it in his hand and wondering what inspired the call.

"How about coming back out to the ranch? We have a need for another wrangler and I understand you have talents in that area. Short term of course. You'll be paid and have the use of one of our cabins."

"I don't know what to say, Mr. MacLaren. It sounds, well, perfect."

"Say yes and we'll consider it a deal."

He raked a hand through his hair and tried to think of any reason not to accept the offer. He came up empty.

"It may take me a few days to arrive."

"No problem. Keep me posted and we'll make sure your cabin is ready."

"All right. And thank you, sir."

Kade tossed his phone on a chair, then reconsidered and picked it up to dial his landlord. He left a message he wouldn't be extending his lease, then called Nesto.

"Hey, man. What's up?"

124

"Heath MacLaren called and offered me a job during my leave."

"No kidding. Doing what?"

"Wrangling." Kade could hear Nesto's laughter and for the first time in days, a smile broke out on his face. "What's so funny?"

"Are you joking? You know how long it's been since you worked horses? Hell, you'll be lucky to come back in one piece. Besides, what about Miss Sinclair?"

Kade sobered at the mention of Brooke. "She arrived in San Diego today. It's doubtful she'll return to the ranch for months, so the timing couldn't be better."

"Sounds like you want to avoid the woman."

"It's more like I have to, mi amigo. I'll be in touch."

******

"Tell me everything. I feel as if I've missed so much while off traveling with my parents." Paige Wallace sat cross-legged on the area rug in Brooke's living room, snacking on pita chips and sipping wine.

"There's not much else. They arrested Perry and I came back here." Brooke's evasive answer had Paige's eyes shining.

She and Brooke had met through Paige's cousin, Shelly, who lived near the naval air base where Brooke's stepbrother, Trey MacLaren, and his wife, Jesse, were stationed. Shelly had been dating Trey's good friend, Ryan "Reb" Cantrell, for a while when Paige drove up to the central California base for a visit. Trey had encouraged her to connect with Brooke, a fellow student at the San Diego university, and they'd been friends ever since.

"And the hunk DEA agent you mentioned?" Paige asked.

"Did I use the work hunk?"

Paige topped off her wine and took a sip. "You didn't have to. I could tell by your description and the look in your eyes. You think the man's hot."

Brooke rested her back against the sofa. "He is a hunk. Way too much of one for me."

"Are you kidding? Any man would jump through hoops to be with you." Paige bristled at the implication some gorgeous man wouldn't be interested in Brooke.

Brooke smiled at her friend's quick defense. "He's an undercover DEA agent, for crying out loud. He rides a chopper, his uniform consists of torn jeans, a leather jacket, and one of those things they wrap around their heads."

"A doo rag," Paige said.

"Right. Anyway, he works nights, never knows where his next assignment will take him, and his companions are drug dealers and people of the worst sort. He lives on the edge, Paige, and I live in a small apartment with my books. I don't even want to know the type of woman he finds attractive." She gulped down the rest of her wine and poured another glass.

"Sure you do." Paige glanced over the rim of her glass, her mind working over possibilities for getting her friend and the hunky agent together.

"Don't even think about going there."

"What?"

"I can see your mind working and it can just stop. He couldn't have been more clear. I'm not the woman for him and I refuse to spend any more time wishing it were different."

"In that case, I believe we should start talking about what type of man would be best for you." She set her glass down and stood, grabbing a spiral notebook and pen before plopping on the sofa. "I'm ready."

"This is ridiculous. I don't need to make a list."

"Of course you do. You have this crazy strong attraction for someone you believe is totally wrong for you. So, what kind of man is right?" Paige asked and settled further into the throw pillows on the sofa.

"Fine, I'll go along for now, but only if I have another glass of wine." Brooke poured one more glass, her last she vowed. She didn't drink much. Somehow the conversation tonight had fueled her need for liquid courage, and why not? The last few weeks had been way beyond anything her staid, academic life ever dished up.

"We know you don't like someone who works nights, ride motorcycles, wears leathers, or has a job requiring travel." Paige wrote as she spoke. "Okay, what else?"

"Nights are all right, just not all the time, and I have nothing against leather or motorcycles." She thought a moment about the last item Paige listed. "Most of the men I've met must do a certain amount of traveling."

Paige scrunched her face. "Help me out here. Should I move these from the con side to the pro side?"

"How about putting a question mark next to them?" Brooke snorted and glanced at her half empty glass. Yep, she should slow down on the wine, or better yet, stop altogether. Already her mind seemed fuzzy and the list Paige insisted on preparing sounded silly. She didn't need a list to know what she wanted.

"I don't think it works that way. If we're going to do this right, you need to be clear about what you do and don't want. How about we list the pros and forget the cons for now?"

"Fine. I want someone who's smart, funny, and doesn't take himself too seriously. He must have good values, work hard, and want a home and children." She glanced at Paige. "How's that?"

"What about attraction or personal chemistry? Don't you want a man who makes your heart race every time he looks at you?" Paige asked.

Brooke tried to focus on the question, but her mind kept latching onto an image of Kade. Tight jeans molded to muscled thighs, arms that felt secure and comforting when wrapped around her, and a deep, rich voice that sent shivers through her body.

"Brooke, did you hear me?"

She tried to shake the image from her mind and found she couldn't. "Sorry. I must be getting tired." She yawned as if to prove her point.

Paige set down the notebook, still open to the page with the half completed list. "It's time I headed home anyway. Let's get together after you're done presenting your research to the committee. And I have the perfect topic for us to discuss—getting you back into the dating scene."

"I'm not certain..." Brooke began only to see Paige disappear outside.

She fell into bed, exhausted, and feeling detached—the way a person feels when they go about their day, moving from task to task, with a sense something is missing. Not an appointment they've forgotten, but more of an emptiness they can't quite identify.

She lay awake, considering the questions Paige had thrown out. Almost a challenge to seek more than a careful, well-planned future, as if her friend knew the flaws in her thinking.

Kade made her feel desirable in ways she'd never experienced. His voice, unique scent, and tender touch ignited sensations beyond what she'd ever imagined and Brooke found herself craving what she knew would never be within her reach. He'd made it clear, there would be no future for them. And she'd agreed.

A long sigh escaped as she made a commitment to push thoughts of Kade aside and concentrate on what life did offer. She'd finish her doctoral program, obtain her designation, and take some much needed time off. Perhaps she'd travel, visit friends around the country, or return to Fire Mountain. For some reason, the last idea appealed to her most. She'd start there, surrounded by those she trusted, and begin a new chapter in her life.

Chapter Nine

"That's the last of it." Nesto placed the final box in the back of Kade's truck. The chopper had been loaded on the trailer, the apartment cleaned, and utilities switched to the landlord. "I guess you're set."

"I'll expect you in a month, and no bull about opting for Hawaii or the Caribbean."

"You know you'll owe me big time if I give up all the chicks on the islands for a bunch of horses and cows." Nesto slapped his friend on the back as Kade climbed into his truck.

"Last I checked, there are women in Fire Mountain, mi amigo, and they're a hell of a lot more your style." Kade slipped on his dark glasses and turned the key. "I'll be in touch."

He hit the interstate, cranked up his tunes, and sat back, trying to remember the last time he'd taken time off. Images of palm trees, the sounds of steel drums, and bikini clad women brought back memories of the time he and Nesto vacationed in Jamaica. They'd both opted not to reenlist, deciding to move into government jobs of another kind. Nesto had three weeks to kill and Kade had two before reporting to their new jobs. Neither turned down any of the bounty available in the island paradise.

Now he headed for rest and recuperation of a different type. This R and R would be nothing like Kade had anticipated when he'd requested the leave several months before.

He had no idea what inspired Heath MacLaren to reach out to him, but the timing couldn't have been better. Working with horses had been his salvation as an angry teenager and given him the confidence he needed to enlist in the Army and later into Special Forces. In a way, it felt as if he were returning to his roots, coming full circle and heading home.

The sun had set behind Fire Mountain when Kade turned his truck and trailer onto the long driveway leading to the main house. This time he returned as a private citizen to work as any other ranch hand instead of in his official capacity as a DEA agent. The difference felt good.

Kade climbed down and stretched, noting the lack of trucks and SUVs which normally clogged the area in front of the house. He looked toward the front door as Heath and Annie walked out.

"I see you made it." Heath extended his hand. He looked past the truck to the trailer which held Kade's chopper. "That's quite a machine."

Kade looked over his shoulder and grinned. "That she is. I've had her for a few years now. Do most of the work myself, although some of the cost is reimbursed by the department."

"You're just in time for supper. Afterwards I'll show you the cabin where you'll be staying. It's not far."

He followed them into the kitchen, surprised to see a young woman standing at the stove.

"Cassie, this is Kade Taylor. He's the man we mentioned who'll be working at the ranch for a few months. Kade, my daughter, Cassie," Heath said.

Annie noticed how Cassie's eyes grew wide at the sight of the strikingly handsome man who stood before her.

"It's nice to meet you Mr. Taylor."

"Pleasure's mine." Kade guessed Cassie to be in her early twenties.

"She attends college in the valley," Annie said as she pulled plates from the cupboard. "It's great when she can get away for a few days and come home."

He vaguely remembered the mention of Heath's children, but neither had been around during his last visit.

"I'll bet it's great to get away." Kade reached out to take the bottle of beer Heath handed him.

"You have no idea." She looked back at the pot on the stove and didn't elaborate.

Kade watched as Annie put an arm around her stepdaughter. "It'll all work out," she whispered.

It didn't take much for Kade to figure out something had happened with Cassie.

Everyone filled their plates and took seats at a small island between the kitchen and formal dining area. Kade liked the setup—informal and comfortable.

"Any updates you can give us on the arrests?" Heath asked.

"Mr. Worton pleaded guilty at his arraignment and is awaiting the next steps. Everyone expects a plea bargain in exchange for his testimony against Paco. It could be a long process. I may need to drive back to attend hearings or provide testimony. Plus there are a couple other pending cases which may need my attention."

"I bet it's be good to be away for a while." Annie picked up her glass of wine.

"It is. I hope it's all right, but I asked a colleague to join me during his vacation. We worked on the same ranch during high school, then entered the Army together."

"Not a problem. Is he with the DEA also?" Heath asked.

"No. Nesto opted for the U.S. Marshal Service. Actually, he and another marshal came here to escort Mr. Worton back to San Diego."

"Buck Towers mentioned a Marshal Salgado," Heath said.

"Ernesto Salgado. He's like a brother."

"Do you have much family?" Cassie asked, contributing for the first time.

"Not really. Growing up it was my mother and me, and a few assorted relatives we didn't see much." Kade fell silent, hoping no one asked any more questions about his family.

"If you're finished, let's get you out to the cabin and settled." Heath grabbed his plate.

"We'll get that, Pop," Cassie said.

"No argument from me."

"Nice meeting you, Cassie. I'm sure we'll run into each other again." Kade grabbed his DEA cap and followed Heath outside.

Cassie's eyes followed him out of sight. "Wow, he's quite the package."

Annie chuckled. "Besides the obvious, he seems like a good man. We didn't learn much about him before as he focused completely on his work.   Well, almost completely."

"What do you mean?" Cassie stood and began to wash off plates.

"I can't swear to it, but there seemed to be a real connection between him and Brooke. Of course, I've been wrong before."

"Not often. You have a knack for noticing links the rest of us miss." She rubbed a hand across her forehead. "Too bad you didn't see the broken link between Matt and me."

"When did he tell you?"

"That's just it, he didn't tell me. He left me a note and followed up with an email a couple of weeks later." She slapped a hand on the counter "A note, Annie. After all the time we were together. He couldn't even tell me to my face."

135

Cassie and Matt Garner had been an item since before she graduated from high school. He was already a sophomore at the local community college and they transferred at the same time to the university in the valley. They were crazy about each other and planned to marry after Cassie graduated. She'd doubled up on classes and had been a semester behind him when he decided he needed a change.

"I didn't even know he'd finished his degree and had been talking to his rodeo coach for months about leaving." She looked up at Annie, her face showing the anger and despair she'd felt over the last few months.

"How long has he been gone?"

"Almost five months." She slumped into a chair. "His coach told me he completed his degree in December."

"Why didn't you tell us before now?" Annie ached for Cassie, who'd been devoted to Matt.

"I thought he'd come back—tell me he'd made a mistake and still loved me. There's been nothing from him since he left. Argh..." Her voice trailed off on a pained groan as she cradled her face in her hands.

Annie placed a hand on Cassie's shoulder. "Have you spoken with his grandfather?"

"Seth's as surprised as I was, and I know he feels terrible about how Matt left." She stood and grabbed a bottle of water from the refrigerator. "I'm sorry to dump all this on you. I just couldn't take being alone another weekend with my roommates out of town."

"Don't be silly. This is exactly where you should be. In fact, you should have come home sooner. I know Heath is steaming about the entire situation. And you know he loves Matt."

Annie took a seat next to Cassie and leaned close. "You know, I never did like that boy."

Cassie's gaze swung to Annie's in shock. Then she saw her stepmother's mouth curve into a slight smile. She let out a pained laugh and took Annie's hand.

"I like that approach. Perhaps if I tell myself I never really liked him, it'll be easier to get over him."

"I don't know if it will be easier, but I do know the pain will subside with time."

Their heads turned at the sound of the front door opening and Heath walking toward them. He took one look at his daughter and the anger he felt at the way Matt had treated her burned all over again.

"Kade get settled all right?" Annie asked.

Heath tore his eyes away from Cassie. "He didn't bring much except clothes, a box of books, and his computer. Oh, and his chopper. It is one of the nicest bikes I've ever seen."

Annie gave him a knowing smile followed by a wink. He'd owned a Harley for several years while he'd been single, making the decision to sell it a few months before he'd met Annie. He had every intention of replacing it with a bigger Harley—he just never got around to it.

"I told him Eric bought another bike—" Heath began.

"He did?" Cassie didn't think he'd ever get another one after his accident while still in college.

"About a month ago."

"Are you okay with it?" Cassie asked Annie.

"It's not my decision. He's an adult and knows the dangers. I'll worry, but I do that anyway."

Cassie grabbed her purse. "I'm bushed. I think I'll head upstairs to bed."

Heath drew her into a hug, like the ones he'd given her when she was little. Cassie wasn't little any longer, yet the hurt she felt now far outweighed the events in her past, and she appreciated his warm, comforting hug.

"Goodnight, sweetheart. Sleep well."

He waited until she'd left before turning to his wife. "I could strangle Matt." He lowered himself into his big well-worn leather chair and scrubbed a hand down his face. "I understand he may have changed his mind about Cassie. But, hell, did he have to do it with a note?"

"He probably couldn't face the way he knew Cassie would react. Matt knows how she loves him and how his decision would devastate her."

"He took the coward's way out."

Annie didn't answer. She loved Matt as if he were another son, had looked forward to him being a part of the family at some point. Now all she felt was heartache for Cassie and confusion over the way Matt handled it. Perhaps in time the reasons would become clear.

******

"Congratulations, Miss Sinclair. By all indications, you've crossed the last hurdle to your doctorate." Dr. Krueger couldn't have been more pleased with the way Brooke handled herself during the presentation and defense of her research. "There may be a few requests for modifications, but overall, you've achieved your goal."

Brooke didn't know what to say. She'd hoped and prayed to get through today without making a complete fool of herself. At Dr. Krueger's suggestion, she'd obtained pre-approvals of her work from each committee member, yet even those personal nods wouldn't have held up if she hadn't been able to defend her work.

"Thank you so much for all of your help and guidance. Also, for accepting my transfer midway through the program." She'd discovered her previous advisor and her ex-fiancé, Perry Worton, had been having an affair for months. Brooke had almost dropped out of the program before her family and friends urged her to find a new advisor and complete her degree.

"You were in a tough situation. I'm glad it all worked out so well."

She waited in the reception area outside the room where the committee had met after her presentation. The wait wasn't long and the congratulations were overwhelming. One professor asked if she planned to celebrate with champagne and someone special. An image of Kade flashed across her mind but she pushed it aside without hesitation. She told the professor what she wanted most was to fall into bed and sleep for a week.

A call to her mother had to come first.

"Hi, Mom. Yes, I just finished and it seemed to go very well. They congratulated me and one referred to me as Dr. Sinclair. Can you believe it?" The achievement had begun to settle in and her voice held a marked tone of excitement.

"That's wonderful news. You've worked so hard for this and we couldn't be more proud. Will you be calling Eric and Cam, or should I?"

"Would you mind calling them? All I want to do now is grab something to eat and fall into bed."

"We'll celebrate as soon as you're able to come home. Do you have any idea of your timing?"

"I've been thinking about it, and for the time being, I plan to stay put. There are a couple of associate professor positions coming up and I may apply for one or both of them."

"I understand. Just let us know when you are able to take off and we'll try to get as much of the family here as possible."

Brooke cringed when she heard the disappointment in her mother's voice.

"I will. As soon as I have a better idea of what's going on."

"Whenever you can get here is fine. We love you Brooke."

"Love you too, Mom. I'll be in touch real soon." She felt bad not being honest about her real plans, but she knew the look on her mother's face when she arrived unannounced, with all her belongings, would be worth it.

******

"I can't believe you didn't call me right away." Paige produced a mock pout as they toasted their frozen caramel macchiatos once more to Brooke's success.

"Truthfully, all I did was go home, make some tea, and fall into bed. I didn't even eat."

"What now?"

"I'm letting go of my place, packing up, and heading home at the end of the month."

Paige's enthusiasm mellowed at her friend's words. "Really? You're going to leave for good?"

Even though Brooke didn't second guess her decision, she knew leaving Paige would be hard. "I need to get out of here for a while. Dr. Krueger urged me to apply for an associate professor position in the management department and I told him I'd think about it. The odd part is, the thought of staying at the university no longer holds any appeal. I hope you understand."

"Of course I understand. That doesn't mean I like it."

"When's your last final?" Brooke asked.

"In two weeks."

"Great. You can come with me. You're between jobs, your parents are traveling in Europe, and you've already told me you have no plans for the summer."

Paige's mouth fell open before breaking into a broad smile. "I'd love to go with you."

"I've given my notice, now all I have to do is pack up and rent a truck. By the end of the month we'll be on our way. I haven't even told my mother what I'm doing. She thinks I plan to stay out here and look for a job. She'll be so surprised."

"Any eligible cowboys at the ranch?" Paige asked.

"Are you thinking of a summer fling?"

"Why not? You forgot to mention I'm also between boyfriends. Other women do it all the time." She leaned forward and lowered her voice. "In fact, we should pick out two. One for each of us."

Brooke shook her head. "Tell you what. I'll help you pick out someone for yourself, but not for me. My plan is to stay in Fire Mountain, maybe work for my stepfather's company, and get involved in the community. I have no interest in a short-term fling or any type of relationship right now. I just want to get settled and try to figure out where I'm supposed to be—at the ranch, back in San Diego, or maybe someplace else. Meeting someone would just complicate everything." Brooke finished her drink and tossed it in a nearby trash bin.

Paige cast an understanding look at her friend. Brooke, more than most, deserved to be part of a great relationship. In her opinion, Perry had been a jerk, and that was before his more recent troubles. Too bad nothing came of her attraction to the DEA agent. She seemed smitten with Kade even if his job didn't fit in with Brooke's plans, or she in his.

Paige leaned in close and touched Brooke's hand. "You know what, we're going to have a great time this summer, with or without hunky cowboys. I can't wait."

******

"Does anyone have any reservations at all about the viability of the purchase?" Heath asked the men gathered in the conference room who'd worked to get the RTC deal this far.

"We already know Chris and Ty want out. Our offer requires all three partners to stay active for the first three months, then taper off until the transition is complete. The idea of having Rafe take over is sound, except who will run the operation if Rafe decides he wants no part of working with MacLaren Cattle?" Colt Minton, the company attorney, had serious reservations about Rafe. He'd known the third MacLaren brother in high school and didn't look forward to the upcoming fireworks which were bound to happen over this deal.

"Jace will work as the interim president if needed. Of course, we're hopeful Rafe will see the benefit of staying. He has the experience, knowledge, and is business savvy. His oldest sons are involved in the operation and I doubt they'll want to quit. It'll be to his benefit to stay." Heath didn't feel as confident as he sounded. It would be a crap shoot either way.

"I'm assuming the offer will be coming from HRJ Enterprises and not MacLaren Cattle." Doug Hester, the company's chief financial officer, thought RTC fit well with the rest of the businesses, although he, like Colt, had serious doubts the deal would ever go through.

"Yes, everything will run through the holding company."

"How do you want to present the offer?" Cam asked.

"You and Doug will fly to Montana—probably the week after next." He pointed at his notes. "The offer is more than fair. I believe Rafe will be the one to up the price or make other demands. Any other questions?" When no one answered, he picked up his folder and stood. "Let's get this going, gentlemen."

"Heath, do you have a minute?" Jace remained seated, waiting as the others left.

"Of course. What's on your mind?"

"Rafe isn't going to be fooled by the HRJ letterhead. If you recall, Pop was forming the holding company at the time Rafe took off, telling us he wanted to make sure the business was left to his three sons."

"I believe he said *three capable sons*."

"You're right, he did. He made it a big deal, champagne, followed by whiskey. I can't image Rafe won't remember." Jace threw his pen on the table and leaned back.

"It's not too late to call it off. One word to Colt and he'll stop drawing up the documents."

Jace walked toward the window, gazing out at hundreds of acres of MacLaren land. "We should've reached out to him years ago when we found out where he'd settled."

"We tried."

"Once, then we let it go when he didn't respond." Jace turned to face his brother.

Heath's mouth curved into a wry grin. "I can guarantee he'll respond this time."

"Yeah. I just hope we're ready."

Chapter Ten

"You're working too hard, Taylor." Jace propped one foot on the bottom rung of the corral fence and rested his arms on the top.

Kade continued hot walking the young gelding. "Are you kidding? This is like a vacation." He'd returned from an hour ride and needed to settle the horse before grooming him.

"When does your friend arrive?" Jace asked. He hadn't been too keen on Heath inviting Kade to the ranch. He'd changed his mind after a few days.

"Tomorrow. Knowing Nesto, he'll want to jump right in."

"He as good as you?"

"Better," Kade grinned and started toward the barn.

Jace followed him inside and rested against one of the stalls, watching as Kade picked up a couple of brushes. "Heath tell you we have company coming in this weekend?"

"His son, I think."

"Trey, his wife, and their son, plus a few of their Navy friends. It'll be a full house. We usually play flag football on Sunday afternoon. Plan on bringing your friend and joining us." Jace strolled from the barn, then turned back. "Come hungry. The women put together a huge spread."

Kade continued sliding the brushes over the horse, talking in soft tones, and admiring the lines. He'd been surprised how quick he transitioned from arresting drug dealers to taking care of horses. The time alone with the animals felt good.

He tossed the brushes in a bucket as the sound of an approaching motorcycle caught his attention. A few minutes later, Eric came strolling inside.

"Time to put that stuff away and go for a real ride." He and Eric had been on several rides over the last few weeks.

"Give me half an hour to grab my bike. I'll meet you back here."

"I'll follow you. No sense wasting a moment. Besides, if I stay around here, mom will get her fangs in me and we might never get away."

"Fair enough."

Kade jumped in his truck and took off toward the cabin. The bike sat ready. He grabbed a jacket, strapped a helmet to the back, and they were off. An hour later, Eric pulled into The Tavern, a sports bar popular with locals.

Eric held to a firm rule—no alcohol when he rode the bike. Kade had spent so much time riding with the outlaw gang, he didn't hesitate ordering a beer. He'd developed the habit of nursing one all night. The others in the gang had never caught on to it as they chugged down one drink after another.

"You hear about the group of riders who tore up Bonnie's last night?"

They each glanced at the bartender and shook their heads. Bonnie's sat in the middle of old town and had been popular with motorcycle groups for years.

"About twenty of them showed up, ready for a brawl. From what I hear, the place is a mess and several bikers got thrown in jail."

"Did you hear what started it?" Kade asked.

"Nope. Guess they'll be heading out as soon as their friends are released. At least I hope so."

"You think that'll be the case?" Eric asked Kade as the bartender turned toward other customers.

"Who knows? I gave up guessing what the clubs would do a long time ago." Kade sipped his beer. He'd been called to testify against the members who'd been arrested during his last case but the trial had been postponed—for the second time.

"Did you hear the news about Brooke?" Eric asked.

"Your mom told me she sailed through her presentation. Looks like you'll be calling her Doctor from now on." Kade had thought of sending her a text or email congratulating her, then thought better of it. She'd accomplished her goal and now her life would turn in a new direction while his...well...he wasn't sure where he'd be a few months from now.

"Mom hoped she'd come out here. Guess she's decided to apply for a couple of positions at the university. Maybe the two of you will run into each other if she stays in California."

"Doubtful. Not too many college professors hang out with undercover agents."

Eric glanced at Kade. "You know, Brooke isn't like most people. She's pretty down to earth."

Kade just stared into his beer mug. He didn't want to talk about Brooke or what a great person she is—he already knew it.

"If you're ready..." Eric threw some cash on the counter.

The sun had already set by the time they turned onto the highway. They'd ridden about five miles when a group of motorcycles pulled out of a parking area and fell in line right behind them. Kade hadn't noticed any jackets indicating if they belonged to a club.

Kade had been in the lead when he and Eric started out. Now he signaled to Eric and dropped behind him, putting a barrier between Eric and the other riders. His senses went on high alert. He had a weapon in his saddlebag, not a good place if he needed it quickly. When nothing happened a mile before the ranch entrance, no trouble having surfaced, he began to relax. They came up to the shopping area, signaled their turn, and pulled away from the group. Kade stopped and watched as the bikes rode past. *Black Wolves*. Not the gang he rode with or had to testify against.

Eric made a U-turn to pull alongside him. "Something wrong with your bike?"

"No, just wanted to check on the group behind us. Guess I'm paranoid."

"Nothing wrong with being careful. Ready?"

"Yeah, let's go."

******

"It's looking like early Sunday morning, Paige." Brooke propped the phone between her ear and shoulder as she packed the last few items of clothing in boxes. "Why don't you be here by seven? We'll get an early start." She punched the speaker button and set the phone down, listening to Paige complain about the early hour. "Yes, I know it's before you usually get up but we'll avoid traffic and be there in plenty of time for supper. Mom usually does something special on Sundays." She smiled at Paige's retort. "Great. I'll see you then."

Brooke took another slow scan of her apartment. Everything was packed except some clothes she'd left out for the trip. Two more days and the university would be history. She felt no regrets about not applying for the teaching opportunities. Dr. Krueger had presented compelling reasons to complete the forms, citing how seldom associate professor positions opened up. She hadn't been swayed.

Brooke changed and drove the short distance to a remote parking area by the beach. Tonight she'd run a few miles, enjoy the sunset, and grab a quick dinner—her last in San Diego. She'd miss the beach, especially in the evenings when the colors of the sunset played against the deep gray-blue ocean. Until the decision had been made,

Brooke didn't realize how much time she spent along the coast, studying, running, and swimming. She planned to take in every last moment.

A few months ago, she started noticing a lone motorcycle parked in the upper lot, the rider always staring in her direction. It happened so often, she began to look for him at each visit. His presence hadn't alarmed her—too many people frequented the stretch of sand where she preferred to throw down her towel. Now she realized the rider had been Kade.

At the time, he'd kept his distance, thinking her guilty of assisting Paco Bujazan and his family. A couple of times she'd thought about walking up the path and introducing herself, asking why he didn't come down and enjoy the view up close. In the end, she'd always talked herself out of it, suspecting he'd think her a crazy blonde.

She tossed her towel on the sand and lowered herself to face the crashing waves. The sky had turned dark and the ocean rough this evening, and she wondered if Kade ever came out and watched as he used to. Foolish thoughts, yet the wish to see him again hadn't lessened. Instead, her thoughts turned to him more often rather than less. If his words hadn't been so firm, so final, if he'd given any hint he'd wanted to see her in San Diego, she would've agreed. No one touched her heart the way Kade Taylor did.

Brooke removed her sweatshirt and took off down the beach, keeping a steady pace. The run would be long tonight. She needed to find a way to push him from her thoughts for good—perhaps sweating him out of her mind would be the key. Tonight would be for saying goodbye to the beach, the sunsets, San Diego, and all it encompassed, including Kade.

******

"Took you long enough," Kade said as he clasped Nesto's hand and pulled him into a quick hug.

"Got a late start. Almost had to postpone the entire trip, but got a reprieve at the last minute." Nesto looked at the cabin and surrounding view. "Quite a setup you have here."

Kade reached into the truck to grab Nesto's bag. "Come on, I'll show you the inside."

Heath and Jace had built six identical two bedroom cabins within a few miles of the main ranch house. All were private, located within a short distance of each other.

"This is great," Nesto said as he laid his cap and keys on a table. "Fireplace, full kitchen, the works. And a view that goes on for miles. Going back to city life may be pretty hard after this, bro."

Kade walked down the wood-paneled hallway. "I'm lucky they offered it to me at no charge. Heath and Jace insisted on paying me for the work I do, but I told them not to bother—I'd send the money back. They haven't brought it up since. Oh yeah, and I kicked the smoking habit. Guess being here has had several benefits." He set Nesto's bag on the bed. "How about a beer?"

"Sounds good. What do you hear about your cases?" Nesto asked.

"Clive Nelson called. He's heard rumors members of Satan's Brethren are asking about me. I'm surprised it took them this long."

"Maybe they thought the charges against those arrested wouldn't stick. Word on the street is it's a pretty tight case—as long as you testify." Nesto took a long swallow of his beer and followed Kade out onto the deck. "Damn nice view." He settled into a wooden lounge chair and propped up his feet.

"I sit out here most nights. A few times I've taken one of the horses out or ridden the bike with Eric Sinclair, Brooke's brother. Usually, though, it's just me and a bottle of Dos Equis."

"And what about Miss Sinclair. Ever hear from her?"

"She's out of it—the Bujazan case and my life. No longer my responsibility to keep tabs on or babysit her."

"That's one baby I'd be glad to keep tabs on." Nesto smirked when Kade shot him a venomous look. "Hey, you had your chance, man, and you blew it."

"We both walked before it went anywhere. Leave it, bro. It's for the best." Kade finished his beer and tossed it in a nearby can, not at all believing walking away from Brooke had been the best decision for him. "Come on. You can help me barbeque the steaks."

******

Heath heard the noise before the front door opened and a crowd of six adults and one little boy paraded inside. Spotting his grandfather, Trevor MacLaren ran and jumped into Heath's waiting arms.

"Glad to see you all made it," Heath said as Trevor began to squirm. He set the boy down and hugged his son, Trey, then his wife, Jesse.

"It's the first time in months we've all been able to get together, what with deployments, and transfers." Trey walked toward his stepmother, Annie, who'd walked through the door with Trevor in her arms. "Looks like he found you."

"Sure did. He's grown so much," Annie said as she gave her grandson a gentle squeeze.

Ryan "Reb" Cantrell and Paul "Growler" Henshaw, both fellow Navy pilots and past visitors to the ranch, walked into the great room with their girlfriends.

"You remember Shelly and Connie," Trey said as the women walked forward. Ryan and Shelly met while he'd been stationed at the large central California naval air base. Paul had met Connie when she'd traveled to visit Trevor, her unofficial godson. Trey, Ryan, and Paul had been roommates at the time.

"Of course we remember them," Annie said. "We're going to have a full house this weekend. I hope some of you don't mind using a couple of the cabins."

"A cabin works great for us." Paul wrapped an arm around Connie's shoulders. He lived in California while she'd flown in from Florida.

"Perfect, because you and Connie have one cabin while Ryan and Shelly have another. Trey, you and Jesse have your old room."

"What about Cassie and Brooke?" Trey asked.

"Cassie drives up tonight. I doubt Brooke will make it. In fact, we haven't heard anything about whether she still plans to stay in San Diego or come out here." Everyone could hear the disappointment in Annie's voice. "All right. Let's get you all settled before supper."

"Ryan and Paul, let's transfer your bags into a couple of trucks. You'll need them to get back and forth from the cabins this weekend." Heath led the way outside while Trey and Jesse stayed behind, following Annie into the kitchen.

"We heard bits and pieces of what went on with Brooke. How's she doing?" Jesse asked.

"Good as far as I know. You already know she finished her doctoral program and they arrested Perry." Annie set an ice tea in front of Jesse, who'd waved off the beer Trey offered.

"I thought she might accept the offer from Dad and Jace to work for MacLaren Cattle." Trey took a long swallow of his beer and sat down next to his wife while keeping an eye on Trevor.

"She still might," Annie said. "Guess we'll have to wait and see. I'd better finish getting dinner ready. Cam and Lainey will be here anytime, along with Eric. Plus we invited a couple of others who are staying at the ranch."

"Who are they?" Trey asked.

"Kade Taylor," Heath said as he walked into the kitchen. "He's the DEA agent who followed Brooke for a couple of months, and his friend, Ernesto Salgado, who's with the Marshal Service. We offered Kade a cabin when Brooke mentioned he'd be taking a leave from his work."

"So he's hanging at the ranch for a while?" Jesse asked.

"He's got another few weeks before he reports back. In the meantime, he's helping with the horses. Taylor and Salgado worked on a ranch during high school and we can always use the extra help." Heath grabbed a beer to match Trey's and leaned against the counter. "I'll be interested to get your opinion of them, especially Taylor."

******

"Come on in," Eric said and held out his hand to Kade and Nesto as they walked in the front door. "Didn't get enough MacLaren abuse on Friday night?" He smiled at the two as they all walked to where everyone sat around talking.

"You've got a long way to go to scare us away." Kade nodded to everyone.

The two had met the rest of the family and friends at dinner a couple nights before. They'd had a great time, learning quickly that no one was spared from the jokes and jabs thrown out.

"Perhaps today's the day," Heath said. "We're assembling teams for our flag football game. You're on my team, Kade, and Nesto's on Jace's. By the way, these are Jace's sons, Blake and Brett. Blake's in college and Brett starts in the fall."

"Nice meeting you," Kade said and shook hands. "When do we start?"

"We're just waiting for a few more—three friends from Cam and Lainey's Search and Rescue team."

Within an hour, the two teams assembled in an open field next to the house, flags hanging from their back pockets, determined looks on each face. Annie flipped a coin and handed the ball to Jace.

"Good luck everyone," she called over her shoulder as she dashed to the sidelines.

They played hard for a friendly Sunday afternoon game. After about thirty minutes, they called halftime, grabbing water, beers, and sodas before digging into the chips, dip, and salsa the women had set out.

"How are you holding up?" Heath asked Kade as both finished their bottles of water.

"Great. I don't know why I thought this would be some wimpy game. These guys are out to win."

"It's the only way we play." Health clasped Kade on the back and turned to the others. "Everyone ready for round two?"

Within a few minutes, the men were back on the field, yelling and laughing as the ball moved back and forth between teams. The intensity increased during the second half.

"All right. This one goes to Kade. See if you can outrun your partner," Heath said, referring to Nesto's ability to catch up to receivers and pull their flag. Kade nodded, aware his friend's bulk belied his agility and quick feet.

"Yeah, the big guy's like a deer dashing around obstacles. Get me the ball and I'll get us some points." Kade's mouth turned up at the corners.

They lined up, Heath called the play, and everyone took off, Kade running toward the end zone while looking behind him for the pass. Heath let go of the ball, but just as Kade's hands claimed it and he turned toward the goal, he spotted a bright red car coming up the drive. The momentary loss of concentration was all Nesto needed to reach him and his flag, tripping Kade in the process. He landed face first with a thud.

"What the hell was that?" Heath mumbled before he too saw the familiar SUV coming into sight. Brooke.

"Appears we got here at just the right time." Brooke smiled at the sight of the familiar Sunday afternoon game. "The guys try to play football each weekend. Looks like more guys than usual."

She glanced at the road, then back at the game, in time to see Heath raise his hand. Brooke tapped the horn twice, drawing the attention of everyone who hadn't already turned to watch her pull to a stop.

Kade stayed on the ground in a sitting position, knees bent with this arms resting on them. The second he'd spotted the car, he knew who was in it. The very person he didn't want to show up and yet the one woman he most wanted to see. He'd have to steel his resolve and stay away from her, for more reasons than she could understand.

Using their jobs as a barrier had been an excuse even if the reasons were sound. The critical obstacle, the one she wouldn't understand, had to remain locked within him, not to be shared with Brooke ever.

Kade watched from a distance as relatives and friends greeted Brooke and another woman he didn't recognize. From this distance, she looked enough like Brooke to be her sister, and Kade noticed, with amusement, Nesto strolling up to them.

"Miss Sinclair. You might not recognize me—"

"Of course I recognize you, Marshal Salgado," Brooke said, holding out her hand.

"Please, it's Ernesto or Nesto when I'm not on duty." He clasped her hand and turned to the other woman. "And you are?"

"Paige Wallace." She turned as a shriek came from the house. Her cousin, Shelly Wallace, ran up and threw her arms around Paige.

"It's so good to see you. I had no idea you'd be here," Shelly said as she dropped her arms and stepped back.

"I didn't know any of you would be here either. This is great."

"Brooke, what's with the trailer?" Cam asked.

Annie stood next to him and Lainey. She didn't dare hope what the trailer might mean.

"I've decided to move here, to the ranch" She glanced at her mother. "If there's room."

Annie threw her arms around her daughter and laughed. "There's always room for you. Heath," she called over her shoulder, "Brooke's come to stay."

He walked over and pulled Brooke into a hug. "I suspected as much when I saw the trailer. Your decision couldn't have come at a better time."

Brooke glanced up at him. "What do you mean?"

"Just a lot going on. Jace and I will explain, but not now. It's time to celebrate, not talk business."

Paige continued to greet the others, all the while keeping watch on the striking man who'd said hello to Brooke. Her breath had caught the moment she'd seen him saunter up to her friend. Even though they had just been introduced, she knew from Brooke's recounting of her ordeal who he was, and his friendship with Kade Taylor. Her gaze traveled toward Brooke, who'd disengaged from the group and appeared to be frozen in place at the back of her car.

Chapter Eleven

Brooke shaded her eyes from the bright sun, wondering about the presence of Ernesto Salgado. She scanned the area, not seeing who she hoped, then walked to the back of her SUV and opened the back. She'd pulled one bag out before a movement to her right caught her attention. She turned, then all further movement stopped as she gazed at the man who'd haunted her thoughts for weeks. His skin held a deeper tan than she remembered and he'd cut his hair, no longer wearing the queue. Dirt covered his face and arms, not at all changing the fact he was still the most compelling man she'd ever met. His torn jeans and snug t-shirt accentuated his achingly perfect body as he continued to move toward her.

"Hello, Brooke."

Had his voice changed? It sounded deeper and rough.

"Kade." Her own voice trembled even as she tried to control it. "I didn't expect to see you here."

"Heath invited me out when he learned about my leave. I'm staying in one of the cabins, along with Nesto Salgado who's taking a two week vacation. I heard you planned to stay in San Diego and not move back. Seems I heard wrong."

Realization dawned. "I see. So you accepted Heath's invitation knowing I wouldn't be around. Makes sense." She turned and grabbed another bag from the car.

Deciding to let the rest wait for later, she began to roll the bags toward the house.

"I'll take that." Kade placed a hand next to hers and drew one bag toward him, keeping pace alongside her.

She felt a jolt at the brief touch of his hand. A memory of their kiss the night they'd said goodbye radiated through her. Brooke found she wanted to turn back time and change what she'd told him. She'd tell him the differences between them didn't matter—nothing mattered except learning more about each other and exploring a relationship. She reminded herself he'd been clear it wouldn't work. Brooke ignored the wave of regret and focused on how she'd be able to deal with his presence during the rest of his stay.

"Congratulations, by the way. I should have called or ..." He shrugged, unsure of what else to say.

She glanced over at him. "Thank you. I'm just glad it's over."

"I guess you'll be staying in the house." Kade knew he should let the conversation die, take the bag inside, and let her visit with family, but an odd feeling of possessiveness took hold at the realization he didn't want to share her time. He wanted Brooke to himself. If he couldn't have her the way he wanted, they might be able to become friends.

"For a while. Heath offered me one of the cabins if I moved to Fire Mountain. As much as I love my family, I think the privacy would be best."

"There she is. We thought you'd already gotten lost." Eric took the bag from Kade, placed it at the bottom of the stairs, then rejoined the others. "Mom's about ready to set out the food. You arrived just in time."

Kade watched the two walk away. The sense of loss he felt at her departure was new and unwelcome. He turned in the opposite direction and walked toward the bar in Heath's study, grabbed the bottle of whiskey and poured a shot. He held it up a moment before tossing it back and letting the warm, amber liquid slide down his throat.

"I thought I saw you disappear in here."

Kade turned at the sound of Heath's voice. "I hope it's okay." He held up the whiskey bottle before pouring one more shot.

"Only if you pour me one." Heath studied Kade. His demeanor had changed the moment he'd spotted Brooke's car. "It's good to have Brooke back, don't you think?"

"Uh, yes. I'm sure you and Annie are happy to have her here."

"We knew whatever decision she made would be the right one, although her mother and I privately hoped Fire Mountain would be her choice." Heath took the glass Kade offered and saluted him with it before taking a sip. "Seems like something's on your mind. You know you're welcome to use me as a sounding board."

Kade hesitated, almost taking Heath up on his offer. Unfortunately, the two problems foremost in his mind were concerns he couldn't discuss with this man, or anyone in the MacLaren family. He had to deal with them himself, in his own way and on his own terms.

"I appreciate the offer, but I'm doing fine."

"Dad, Annie needs your help." Trey stood in the doorway, holding Trevor's hand.

"Appears I've been summoned. Remember, my offer stands if you ever want to unload."

Kade nodded as Heath left and Trey closed the distance between them.

"I've been meaning to thank you for keeping track of Brooke and not letting her get caught up in the Bujazan web. She's smart, although she can be much too trusting for her own good."

"I doubt she'd recall my presence as protective." One corner of Kade's mouth quirked upward as he rested a hip against the desk. "You know we were trying to build a case around the son and thought she figured into the deals. I didn't believe her to be an innocent bystander."

"Doesn't matter. You figured it all out and arrested Perry. He's a worthless piece of..." Trey's voice trailed off as he looked down at Trevor. "Well, you know what I mean."

"That I do."

"Our group will be taking off after supper. It's been good to meet you, Kade. Perhaps we'll run into each other again."

"Perhaps we will, Trey," Kade said, although he doubted it would happen. He didn't regret the decision to spend his leave at the ranch. He'd even fantasized about asking Heath for a full-time job, leaving the DEA and any other law enforcement job behind. The option disappeared with the arrival of Brooke.

******

"It seems so quiet around here with Trey and his group gone." Brooke bit into her cinnamon raisin bagel covered in cream cheese and glanced at Paige, who slathered butter on hers.

"I'm so glad we made it in time to see them. Shelly and I haven't gotten together in months what with my school and her work. I didn't know she and Reb were still together, or Paul and Connie." She took a bite of her bagel and chased it with a swallow of coffee. "What are the plans for today?"

"How about a ride?"

"Sounds great, although you'll have to prep me a little. It's been years since I've ridden."

"No problem. I need to grab my boots and hat. Let's meet downstairs in fifteen minutes." Brooke rinsed her plate and dashed to her room, finding what she sought in the corner of her closet. She attached a small knife to her belt before grabbing handkerchiefs for herself and Paige. You never knew when a dust storm might kick up. She headed downstairs to find Paige already waiting, talking with Annie.

"You're welcome to come with us," Paige said as Brooke walked up.

"Thanks, but I have some appointments. Do you know where you'll be going?"

"I thought we'd head toward the cabins so I can show Paige the one where I'll be staying. I'm getting real excited about it, Mom."

"You can have your pick, any cabin except the one Kade is using. He's got a couple months left until his leave is up and I figure you'll want to move into yours before then. You can't miss his. Just look for the chopper."

The mention of Kade caused a tightening in her chest, while the thought of moving into a cabin near him sent a brief jolt of panic through her body. Although the cabins had privacy, sitting on a few acres each, you could still see the structures, and hear cars coming and going. She'd have to pick one as far away from his as possible or wait to move into a cabin until he returned to his job in California.

Brooke followed Paige outside, walking toward the corral next to the barn where Gremlin grazed near the fence. Another horse stood several feet away.

"Those are the horses we'll take. First I need to grab their halters." She pulled two sets of gloves from her back pocket and handed a pair to Paige. "You'll want to wear these." Brooke got to the barn entrance before the sound of voices coming from inside caught her attention. She recognized them right away and took a deep breath, determined not to let Kade know how he still affected her.

"Good morning, Kade, Nesto." She noticed two horses already saddled and ready to go. It appeared the two men had the same idea.

Kade turned at the sound of her voice, letting his eyes wander from her shiny boots to her tight fitting jeans, and up to the well-worn brown hat, before settling on her face. His gaze locked with hers and Brooke saw a hint of appreciation before he shifted his stance and looked toward Paige.

"You two are up early. Looks like you plan to ride." Kade took a couple of steps forward, careful to keep his distance from his greatest temptation.

"Yes." Brooke cleared her throat and tried again. "I want to show Paige the cabins and some of the ranch."

"Tell me which horses and I'll get them." Kade grabbed two halters.

"No problem. I can get them."

"Nope, that's not how it works. Heath is paying me to help with the horses and the job includes getting the horses ready to ride. Now, which horses should I bring in for you?"

"Gremlin and Daisy. Thanks."

Kade tossed a halter to Nesto and the two exited out the rear double doors. Within a couple of minutes they strolled back in, leading the horses to a spot close to the tack area.

"Show me the saddle and tack you prefer." Kade's eyes held a hint of mischief, as if he knew something she didn't.

"This saddle and the snaffle bit hanging on the saddle horn for Gremlin, and the saddle and bit next to it for Daisy." She hadn't had someone saddle her horse for her since she first came to the ranch after her mother married Heath.

The women stood aside as the men made quick work of saddling the horses and leading them outside. Kade handed Gremlin's reins to Brooke while Paige took Daisy's from Nesto.

"We're heading out also. Do you mind if we join you?" Nesto asked Paige, certain Kade would never ask Brooke.

"That would be great, don't you think so, Brooke?" Paige jumped at the chance to get to know more about Nesto.

A pained expression crossed Brooke's face before she hid it with a weak smile. "Sure, if that's what they want to do."

"Perfect, right, Kade?" Nesto didn't wait for a response before walking inside to grab the reins to his horse.

Kade looked at the ground and shook his head enough so Brooke knew he felt the same way she did about spending time together. It was a bad idea. "I'll get Blackjack."

The four took off with Nesto claiming a spot next to Paige, leaving Kade to either partner with Brooke or ride alone, making their desire to distance themselves from each other even more obvious. Brooke edged Gremlin forward, ahead of Paige and Nesto, one part of her hoping Kade would stay at the rear, another part wanting him next to her.

"Let's head over the hills then drop into the valley. Sound good?" she asked Kade when he pulled alongside her.

"You're the leader, I'm just following along." Kade's mouth remained set in a thin line.

They rode for a couple of miles, neither saying a word, not even attempting small talk. Brooke noticed the way Kade settled into the saddle and his relaxed posture, a signal of how comfortable he felt on the horse.

She glanced behind her to see Paige and Nesto chatting and laughing—obviously having a great time. Before long, Brooke decided she'd had all she could take of the silence.

"Do you usually ride Blackjack?"

He didn't look her way or change the dour expression he'd worn since they left the ranch. "A few times a week."

She waited for him to continue. When he didn't, she tried again.

"Do you exercise all the horses?"

"The ones kept at the ranch."

She mentally tallied the number. "About a dozen?"

"Closer to twenty between the ones in the stables and those in the corrals. Cassie likes them warm for the lessons she gives when she's home from college, so I work around her schedule."

Wow. More than a few words. He must be loosening up.

"What else are you doing for Heath?"

This time he swung his head toward her, his eyes sharp and compelling. "Whatever he asks, Brooke."

His response took her aback, all the friendliness he'd shown the day before gone. She turned her head away, receiving his message loud and clear—he had no interest in small talk, not with her anyway.

******

What the hell was wrong with him, Kade thought when he saw the look of surprise and hurt on Brooke's face. He'd decided yesterday there might be a way they could be friends, and not push the barriers he knew had to be in place. The issue was his body's instant reaction to her, which he could find no way to defend against, except by pushing her away.

In San Diego, while she remained a suspect and he'd been watching her movements, he used to follow her to the beach. She'd run, read, or just sit watching the sunset. It didn't matter. He'd wanted her as much then as now, except there had been an impenetrable line between them—his DEA credentials and her status as a possible suspect. Sometimes, after she'd leave, he'd follow until certain she'd settled into her apartment for the night. Afterwards, he'd return to the beach and run or go for a swim—anything to cool his aching body. Even then, his

170

mind would wander, envisioning the two of them sitting on the water's edge, enjoying the sound of the crashing waves and the glow of the setting sun. No other woman had ever affected him in such an extreme way.

"Hey, compadre? When do we reach our destination?" Nesto rode up beside him and Kade hadn't even heard him approach. He was losing his touch.

"The cabins are around the next bend. I don't know which one she has in mind, so we'll just follow her until she stops at one."

"Good enough." Nesto reined back and waited for Paige to catch up.

At least those two were enjoying the ride, Kade thought. He watched as Brooke rode ahead, and although her back remained straight, he could see the slump in her shoulders which hadn't been there before he'd been such a jerk. He tapped Blackjack with his heel, moving him forward and made the decision to get himself under control before he lost all chance of earning her friendship.

******

"This is the one." Brooke reined to a stop in front of a cabin about a half mile from Kade's and slid off Gremlin. "I've always liked the setting. Lots of trees and a view of Fire Mountain." She turned her smile toward Paige, ignoring Kade as she'd done the last part of their ride. "Come on. We'll go inside."

171

She pulled out the master key her mother had provided and turned the lock, motioning for the others to follow.

"This is great. Much larger than I anticipated." Paige walked to the kitchen. "Geez, this is better than my place." Paige's parents had purchased her a two bedroom condo near the school. A nice place in a complex of over two hundred residences.

"I'll show you the bedrooms."

The women took off down the hall, leaving Kade and Nesto to mill about in the living room.

"It's setup like yours, except the furniture is different." Nesto pushed his hands in his pockets and walked to the front windows. "She's right. It's an incredible view."

Kade wandered up beside him and crossed his arms. "How are you getting along with Paige?"

Nesto's gaze shifted to Kade. "Fine. Why?"

"Seems neither of you have stopped laughing since we left the ranch."

"Jealous?"

"Stuff it," Kade muttered as Brooke and Paige joined them near the window.

Nesto turned toward Paige. "Will it work for you?"

"Are you kidding? This place is perfect. Is it anything like the one you two have?"

"An exact duplicate. Let's take a look outside." Nesto held the door open for Paige to pass, then shut it, noticing neither Kade nor Brooke had moved an inch.

Kade turned toward Brooke and let his arms drop to his sides. "Look, about what I said—"

"Forget it. I have." She began to walk outside when she felt Kade touch her arm.

"I'm sorry, all right? I was out of line and..." He searched for the right word.

"Surly?"

His mouth tilted up in a slight curve. "Yeah, that works."

"Look, Kade. I know you don't want anything to do with me and never expected I'd show up here. It's all right. I'll do everything I can to stay out of your way and hope you'll do the same." This time she did walk out the door, leaving him to stare after her.

The outcome wasn't what he expected or wanted, but perhaps it was for the best, he thought, as he stepped onto the porch. The others were yards away, making their way down a path toward a rock outcropping. He'd ridden his bike past this place a couple of times, never stopping even though the tranquil setting intrigued him. The other cabins seemed empty, deserted—this one sent out a unique aura. Peaceful, as if it were at rest, or waiting for the right person to fill it.

"Kade." Nesto waved at him. "Come on down here. You've got to see the view from these rocks."

He nodded and started down the path, his reluctant steps underscoring the unease he felt. Riding with the women had been a mistake. Nesto's vote would be different. He saw the way his friend kept watch on Paige, following her movements, and continuing a running conversation. The man appeared smitten, no doubt about it, which didn't bode well for the next two weeks.

Chapter Twelve

"Here's the complete offer in writing. Of course, we'll give you time to think about it." Heath handed Brooke an envelope. He and Jace had already gone over the terms, responsibilities, required travel, and living arrangements, anticipating her questions.

"Everything sounds perfect and, to be honest, I can't imagine finding anything more challenging. The only issue is when you'd want me to start. Paige plans to be here for a few weeks, and I'd hope to take a little time off. Would the end of summer work?"

Brooke had a hard time containing her excitement. The university could never match the salary Heath and Jace offered, and the projects they'd outlined played to her strengths in operations and systems management. She'd start by preparing an analysis of each separate MacLaren business, preparing a plan for integration, and presenting her recommendations to the board. Then the real work would begin.

She had no illusions about her status as being part of the MacLaren family. It had gotten her in the door, but nothing more. Going forward, she would be judged on her performance, the same as every other employee. If she didn't cut it, she'd be looking for a new job.

"How about September 1st?" Jace asked.

"Perfect." She glanced at the envelope in front of her, already knowing its contents, and felt a lump build in her throat. Her life seemed to be coming together. She looked to Jace, then Heath. "I don't need to think about it. I'm honored to have this opportunity. September 1st it is."

"That's great news and perfect timing. Annie insisted on preparing a meal to celebrate you coming on board." Heath chuckled remembering the look on his wife's face when he told her they'd be making Brooke an offer.

"When?" Brooke asked.

"Tonight."

Brooke shook her head. "It's just like her to already know what my answer would be." She stood and shook hands with both men before picking up the paperwork. "Paige and I will see you tonight." She turned toward the door.

"By the way, Kade and Nesto will be joining us." Heath threw this out as if it weren't any big deal.

"That's great. The more the merrier," Brooke mumbled as she closed the door behind her, not at all pleased about a celebration dinner that included Kade Taylor.

******

"Come on in. We're all in the kitchen." Eric stepped aside to let Kade and Nesto pass by him.

"She accepted their offer, huh?" Kade asked.

"She sure did. It's not a real surprise. Heath and Jace are generous in their offers."

"And their expectations are high for those who accept," Kade said.

Eric turned toward him. "There are a lot of challenges running a large corporation with multiple entities. Most people don't realize the extent of the MacLaren businesses. They put a microscope to Brooke's education and experience consulting with large companies while in her doctoral program. She has what they're looking for and will expect her to deliver or she'll be gone—just like any of us would be if we didn't perform. Now," he clasped Kade on the shoulder. "Let's get something to drink."

"Ah, there they are. I wondered when you two would show up." Heath turned back to Jace to say something before walking toward Kade and Nesto. "Have you been keeping yourselves busy?"

"Oh, yeah. Staying busy doesn't seem to be a problem around here." Nesto accepted the beer Eric handed him and let his eyes scan the room before seeing Paige in the hall with Brooke and Cassie. She turned and smiled as her gaze landed on him.

"Cassie had a few additional horses delivered today. She's planning a trail ride this weekend with her student riders and wants me to check out the horses—make sure they're okay for inexperienced riders. She asked if we'd be able to go along." Kade shifted a little so he could keep an eye on Brooke, who still stood with Paige and Cassie.

"It's a good idea to have you along on the ride. I believe Brooke and Paige are also going. Three days and two nights, as I recall." Heath leaned against a nearby chair and wrapped an arm around Annie who'd come up to stand next to him. "Do you know where she plans to go?"

"We'll trailer the horses about fifteen miles north of here and set up a base camp. She has routes established for both Saturday and Sunday morning, then we'll pack up and come back. The students will carpool to the base camp, which will make it a little easier." Kade glanced again toward Brooke and saw her eyes jerk from his direction to focus back on something Cassie said, indicating she knew he was there. "I didn't know Brooke and Paige would be coming. I'll need to plan for their horses as well. Looks like Nesto, Blake and I will each be driving a trailer."

Blake MacLaren was Jace's oldest son, a university student who'd come home for the summer. He'd been working with his father at their company headquarters until Jace had partnered him with Kade and Nesto the previous day to help get the horses ready for the trail ride.

"Sounds good. The three of you along with Cassie, Brooke, and Paige should be enough to work with the less experienced riders." It would also provide for some interesting campfire stories, Heath thought as he pulled Annie a little closer to his side.

"I came to tell you supper's about ready," Annie said as she dropped her arm from around Heath's shoulder. "I'd better let the others know."

"If you'll excuse me, Heath, I'd like to congratulate Brooke." Kade said hello to several others as he made his way across the room. He saw her glance up then look away as if to warn him off. Well, he thought, it won't work.

"Hey, Kade, how's it going?" Cassie asked as she stepped aside to let him stand next to Brooke, while Nesto edged in beside Paige.

"Good. Busy with the new horses." Kade glanced at Brooke, who lowered her gaze when their eyes met. He needed to find a way to speak with her alone and set things right. "They're a good group of horses. Where'd you get them?"

"From our breeding stock program run by Jace and his men. We ship horses all over the country for different purposes." Cassie watched as Brooke shifted from one foot to another, looking uncomfortable.

"I think I'll get another drink," Brooke said and turned to leave.

"I'll go with you." Kade stayed with her for a few feet then placed a hand on her arm. "Do you have a minute to talk?"

"Now?"

"Or after supper. It doesn't matter, but I'd like some time with you."

Brooke looked around to see Annie herding everyone toward the table.

"After we eat would be best."

"Works for me. Thanks."

Brooke gave a brief nod before following the others, while trying to calm the butterflies in her stomach. She'd started feeling edgy the moment Kade had entered the house. No matter how determined she tried to be about forcing her feelings aside, she couldn't seem to overcome her body's natural reaction to the man. Just the sight of him was enough to affect her, no touching or talking necessary. His mere presence triggered unwanted and uncontrollable responses foreign to anything she'd ever experienced.

Brooke found a place at the table and set her glass down as Kade pulled out her chair and took a seat beside her. This time her heart rate picked up, tapping a strong beat she could feel throughout her body. She wanted Kade in a way that frightened her. Self-control had always been a strong asset for her, yet around this man, it melted away. Every fiber in her being wanted to lean over and kiss him, right in front of everyone. The thought of acting on the impulse terrified her.

"Thanks," she said, her voice almost a whisper.

"What do you want?" Kade asked.

"Want?" Her eyes shot up to his, and panic filled her. Had he read her mind?

"You know, to drink?"

"Oh…water for now. Thanks." Brooke settled into her chair and took a deep breath. She had to get control. Now, before anyone noticed her uneasiness with Kade and commented.

"He is something, isn't he? Smart, educated, good with animals, a gentleman, and your classic male heartthrob." Cassie took a seat on Brooke's other side, her eyes following Kade to the counter where he poured two glasses of water. "But, all this is old news to you, right?"

Brooke swallowed hard. "I don't know what you mean."

"Cut it out, Brooke. We may not have spent tons of time together, but it's pretty obvious to me you two have something going. Or, want to. Right?" Cassie watched him approach. "Never mind, he's here. We will talk later, though."

Brooke felt like sliding under the table. If Cassie thought something was going on between her and Kade, then others might, too, and it wasn't the case. To her great disappointment, there was nothing except casual conversation and a thinning thread of friendship.

"Here you go." Kade set her glass down and took a seat, noticing Nesto across the table next to Paige. "Seems those two are getting pretty chummy." He looked at Brooke and nodded across the table.

"They seem to have it hit it off very well. It wouldn't surprise me if they stayed in touch once Paige goes back to school. He's based in San Diego, right?" Brooke envied the easy connection Paige had made with Nesto, and wished she could find some way of establishing a comfort zone with Kade. As it stood right now, she found they had no middle ground.

"Yes. As I understand it, he can keep San Diego as his base for a long time, maybe his entire career with the Marshal Service. He has no reason to put in for a transfer, so my guess is he'll stay there." He glanced at Brooke, wishing he could lean over and kiss her. Not a sweet peck on the check, but a full assault on those beautiful, lush lips that had tempted him since she'd first come home. She shifted her gaze to his and licked her lips in an unconscious gesture, triggering a groan from Kade.

"Sounds like you're hungry," Brooke commented.

"Yeah, starving," Kade answered, knowing the type of hunger he felt had nothing to do with food.

Brooke filled her plate and passed the dishes to Kade. He piled the food high, as if he hadn't eaten in a week and she found herself smiling as he dug in.

"This is great," he said between mouthfuls. "Did your mom make it all?"

"It's always a team effort. Caroline, Cassie, Lainey, Paige, and I all helped. It's a great female bonding experience," she quipped.

"Lainey's here, but not Cam. He isn't in town?" Kade asked.

"He's still in Colorado the rest of the week handling the bronc stock business Heath and Jace bought a few months ago. They've got him involved in so much, I don't know when he and Lainey have any time together."

"Which reminds me, congratulations on your new job." He finished eating and pushed his plate away.

She shot him one of her gorgeous smiles that made his breath catch.

"Thanks. I think I'm still in shock—it's such a great opportunity."

"Are you finished with your dinner?" His voice, thick and unsteady, sent chills through her.

"Yes."

"Good. Let's get out of here for a little bit." He pulled out her chair and rested his hand on the small of her back as they walked outside.

The temperature had dropped to a comfortable sixty-eight degrees as the sun passed behind the mountains, leaving a slight glow in the sky. It wouldn't be long before the light faded and they'd be pitched into darkness, except for the light of the stars and partial moon.

Kade guided her toward a corral where several horses grazed in the waning sunlight. He leaned on the top rail, resting his arms and placing one boot on the lower rung. Brooke stopped beside him and stepped onto the fence with both feet, allowing her to look over the top rail.

"Are those the new horses Callie mentioned?"

"They are. We'll be using them this weekend for the trail ride. Are you looking forward to it?" Kade asked. He kept his eyes straight ahead, not allowing her to see the interest in them.

"I am, and Paige can't wait. She's never been on a ride longer than a couple of hours, so this will be a real experience for her."

He took a slow breath, making a decision to address the wide chasm between them.

"Brooke, about before—"

"It's all right, Kade. We both know the odds of anything working out between us are slim." She stepped to the ground and looked up at him. "I must admit, though, sometimes it's hard for me to remember the reasons." Her mouth curved into a thoughtful smile.

He could see the desire in her eyes and worked to hold himself in check. Reaching out to pull her toward him would be the worst move right now.

"Anyway, your life is in California and I'll be starting over here. We made the right decision."

"You think so?" His voice had grown thick with a tinge of regret.

She looked away, deciding whether to be truthful or say what she thought he'd want to hear. She'd never been any good at avoiding her feelings.

"No." Her eyes locked on his a brief moment before shifting away.

He choked out a grim laugh. "I don't either."

Brooke absorbed his words, wondering why they fought so hard to stay away from each other when each felt so drawn to the other. Was attraction and desire always this complicated?

Kade turned away from her and started walking toward the barn. She fell in step next to him and waited.

"The assignment inserting me into the biker gang changed how I view people. I thought I'd seen it all in Afghanistan during my time in Special Ops, but the people in those gangs are a step below anything I'd ever witnessed. I rode with them for two years, knowing, going in, it would be dangerous work. That's probably why I took it. I've always lived on the edge and this was another opportunity to continue the pattern." He fell silent as they approached the barn entrance and moved toward Blackjack's stall.

"Do you want to talk about what you saw?"

"Not tonight." He gazed at the big, black stallion. Kade found he never tired of looking at the magnificent animal, or at the beautiful woman beside him. "The odds are pretty good I'll be testifying against those we arrested. I'm looking forward to it and hope they don't agree on some type of plea bargain."

"Would you do it again? Go back into a gang for months or years?"

He thought a moment, already knowing the answer, yet not sure how much to say. "Right now, I'll just say my future is open. Being at the ranch has brought me back to a life I thought I'd walked away from years ago. Now I'm not so certain."

Brooke's heart raced. If he left the DEA, making a decision to return to working horses, perhaps Heath could find a place for him here. She fought the hope which grew at his words.

"If you quit, and came here, then..." her words drifted off.

He knew what she implied and turned toward her, lifting a hand and stroking it down her cheek before letting his arm drop to his side.

"There's more to it than my job, Brooke. Other issues that can't be dealt with so easily."

"Such as?"

"Stuff in my background. Things I can't change that have nothing to do with what job I have or where I live. Obstacles between us I have no idea how to overcome." His voice was rough and bitter.

Brooke reached out and laid a hand on his arm, squeezing lightly. When he didn't back away, she stepped closer, moving her hand up to his shoulder and reaching up to kiss his cheek. His reaction surprised her.

In one quick movement he'd wrapped his arms around her, pulling her flush to him and crushing his mouth to hers. The calm she'd felt a moment before shattered at the intensity and hunger of his kiss. His tongue traced her full lips, then slipped inside to explore further as his arms tightened around her.

She circled his neck with her arms, threading her fingers through his hair, while aligning her body to his. She could feel every taut muscle and strained to get closer, letting out a soft moan as his hands moved up and down her back, creating a heat like nothing she'd ever known. The kiss went on and on, sometimes gentling before returning to an almost desperate ravishing of her mouth. Finally, she could feel the intensity decrease and his grip begin to loosen.

Kade raised his mouth from hers, and gazed down, his deep green, passion filled eyes betraying the desire he felt. He wanted to continue, with more than just kisses, yet he knew it would be a mistake.

He dropped his arms and stepped back. "We'd better go back inside." His raspy voice broke as he grabbed her hand and started for the house.

She pulled him to a stop a few yards from the front door and forced him to look at her.

"Why can't this work, Kade?" Her shaky words broke the silence.

He ran a hand through his hair and looked away, not ready to meet her gaze. In his mind, there existed substantial problems Brooke would have no way of understanding. If he told her, there wasn't a shred of doubt in his mind her feelings toward him would change. He couldn't chance seeing the disillusionment in her eyes if she learned the truth.

"Let it go for tonight, Brooke. Please." He leaned down and brushed his mouth over hers, fighting the urge to pull her toward him again.

"Ah, there you two are."

Kade took a step back as Nesto and Paige walked outside to join them. Even though Kade kept his face impassive, he could see the knowing look in Nesto's eyes.

"Your family's asking about you, wondering where you and Kade went." Paige's eyes glittered, sensing something had changed between Brooke and Kade, yet she saw no sense of joy on either face.

"Nesto's going to show me the new horses, then we'll be back inside."

"We should take off once you're done," Kade said to Nesto. "Early day tomorrow."

"Don't forget, you promised to help Brooke move into the cabin," Paige reminded the men.

Kade looked at Brooke. "We didn't forget. Will tomorrow after lunch work?"

She nodded, still reeling from what may be happening between her and Kade. After what transpired in the barn, and the comments he made, she refused to let whatever had started between them die. She'd get him to talk and find a way to make it work.

"I'd better get inside before they come looking for me." She wrapped her hand in Kade's as Paige and Nesto turned toward the pasture.

Chapter Thirteen

"Everyone ready?" Cassie asked as she walked by each horse trailer toward her cousin Blake, who sat behind the driver's seat in the last truck. She'd be riding with him, Paige with Nesto, and Brooke with Kade. They figured it would take about two hours on a Friday afternoon to reach base camp, unload the horses, and finish the final set up before the students arrived around suppertime.

"We're set," Kade called and climbed into his truck, glancing at Brooke. She'd pulled her hair into a ponytail, covered by a baseball cap sporting an Arizona Diamondbacks logo. Blake refused to let her ride with them until she'd replaced the San Diego Padres cap she'd shown up wearing. She looked happy—and young.

Kade drove toward the main highway before taking a couple of turns onto an old trail leading to their base camp on MacLaren property. They'd used this location many times for trail rides with family and groups of new riders. Cassie had been giving lessons since high school, as well as summers during college, and she had a standard routine for the two days of riding.

"You must be busy setting up the cabin. I haven't seen you at the house the last couple of days." It had surprised Kade how disappointed he'd felt when Brooke hadn't been by the house since moving her belongings into the cabin. Paige had stopped by a couple of times, mainly to visit Nesto, he suspected, while Brooke stayed behind.

"Dr. Krueger and the committee asked me to make a few more revisions to my thesis. Small items, but they took time. I hope it's their last request for changes." She rolled down the window, turned off the air conditioning, and let the fresh breeze fill the cab. "There's nothing like the smell of pine trees." She flashed a brilliant smile his way. The impact was immediate as he felt all the air being sucked from his lungs.

"It is beautiful up here." Kade's soft words reflected his feelings about the view inside as well as outside. He drove another mile then pulled to a stop, allowing enough room for the other two rigs. Without another word, he jumped from the truck and walked to the back of the trailer. He needed space. Having Brooke so close had been more than a small temptation. He had to keep reminding himself of the valid reasons why they couldn't have a relationship even as his body, and heart, protested his reasoning.

"What can I do?" Brooke asked as she came around the back.

"Why don't you and Paige help get everything out for supper and store your gear? I believe Cassie said the three of you will be staying in the tent over there," he said, pointing a few yards away.

"I could help you first—"

"No need. I've got this covered."

She took the hint, even though his obvious dismissal stung. Brooke found he ran hot, then cold. He wanted her, no doubt in her mind, and she wanted him. Whatever bothered him about a relationship with her ran deep. She'd lain awake the last few nights dissecting the situation every way she could before making the decision to find a way to get him to open up and talk to her.

The first of the students arrived a few hours later, the excitement obvious on their faces. Most were high school age, a couple in their twenties, and one older couple whose children were grown and out of the house. They'd given up their horses years ago when they no longer had a place to keep them. Neither needed lessons but kept going to Cassie for the opportunity to ride. Cassie had long since stopped charging them.

"Hey. I'm so glad you could make it." Cassie walked up to the older couple and gave each a hug. "I've got a tent set up for you in those trees. Go ahead and get comfortable. The food should be ready soon."

Blake, Brooke, and Paige helped the others get settled while Kade and Nesto handled the horses. Eight students plus the six of them—a good ratio even though Paige had less experience than most everyone else.

Kade kept an eye on Brooke without attempting another conversation. Guilt gnawed at him for the way he'd cut her off earlier. He hung onto his self-control by a thread, knowing he had little resistance when it came to her. He had never felt this way before, allowing a woman to dominate his thoughts, and weaken his ironclad restraint. He'd been known for his steadfast resolve during his time in Special Ops and as a DEA agent, yet it alluded him whenever Brooke came into sight. Frustration didn't even begin to describe how he felt about it.

"All right, everyone. Please gather around the fire so we can go over the plans for tomorrow." Cassie pulled up a camp chair. Supper had gone well with everyone appreciating the stew, biscuits, and pie. Now they had to get down to business. "We all ride together. I'll be in the lead with Blake," she nodded toward her cousin, "taking up the rear. You've all met Kade and Nesto. They'll be riding up ahead and between riders, checking to be sure all is okay and no one is having any problems. Please let one of us know right away if you or your horse is having any problem." She continued on for several minutes before opening the discussion up for questions.

Brooke watched as Kade took a seat on an old log on the other side of the campfire from her, stretching out his long legs and listening to Cassie. Within minutes, two young women took seats on either side of him. Both appeared to be in their early twenties, and quite attractive. Brooke cringed as he talked and laughed with them, wishing he'd chosen to sit by her.

Nesto and Paige sat together a few feet away, their hands entwined. Brooke wondered about the progress of their friendship, but hadn't asked. Now she didn't have to. She looked back toward Kade and noticed he and the young women had disappeared.

"Well, if there aren't any other questions, you're free to wander around, but don't go too far from camp. The ride will start right after breakfast tomorrow." Cassie closed her spiral notebook, stood, and started toward Brooke. "Are you okay? You don't look so good."

"I'm fine. A little tired and ready for bed. Do you mind if I head into the tent now?"

"Not at all. I won't be far behind unless some of the students want to stay up and talk." Cassie turned back to some of the others who still sat around the fire.

Brooke let her eyes sweep the campsite, looking for Kade and the two women. She knew there would be a logical reason they were off together. She decided not to let herself dwell on where they'd gone as she grabbed a bottle of water and headed toward her tent.

She'd been a fool during her engagement to Perry, never suspecting he'd been having an affair for months before walking in on him with another woman. Later she'd discovered it hadn't been his first. He'd been known around the university for his numerous sexual conquests and she'd never had a clue. Every time she thought of how blind she'd been, she wanted to scream.

Brooke dropped down on her sleeping bag, pulled off her boots, and laid back, resting an arm across her eyes. She had no claim on Kade, yet the thought of him being attracted to other women hurt, and not just her heart. It had taken her a long time to regain her self-respect after Perry. She had no wish to lose it again.

"Cassie told me I'd find you in here. Is it all right if I come in?" Kade's voice rousted her from the pity party she'd been having.

She sat up and pushed the hair from her face. "Sure. I'd offer you a seat, but as you can see, there aren't any."

He chuckled and sat cross-legged at the end of her bedroll. He'd followed the two women to their tent to help them get their lantern working. As he'd left their tent, he'd spotted Brooke scanning the area, certain she'd been searching for him.

"Two of the gals needed help with their lantern," Kade said, more to gauge her reaction than for any other reason.

"And you're telling me this why?"

Amusement crinkled the corners of his eyes. "No reason. Just thought you'd be interested."

She glanced at him, and seeing the humorous look on his face, smiled. "Well, they went to the right man."

He remained seated, not knowing what else to say and not wanting to leave.

"Cassie has you riding out front tomorrow. Like a scout."

"We called it taking point in the military. Of course the job meant something entirely different in Special Ops."

"Was it difficult, your job in the military?" She leaned on an elbow and stretched her legs out, touching his thigh with her feet. He picked one up and started to massage it.

Slow, deep, movements sending a tingling feeling throughout her body.

"Not difficult because we knew what had to be done and were trained for it. We just didn't know when we'd be sent out. Special Ops had a different way of operating from the standard Army. Our assignments were sanctioned yet few knew the details. We weren't told much until right before each mission." He continued to massage her foot, enjoying the way a slight moan would escape as he'd change pressure or location.

"Do you miss it?" Her voice had grown rough, husky.

"No. I had no problem doing my job while in the service, but the time had come to try something else. Too many politicians with no military experience making decisions that should have been made by people trained to make the difficult, life and death decisions that arise in the heat of battle, people with hands-on experience. Bureaucrats should never be in charge of military operations. They have different goals from the fighting forces—primarily the desire to be reelected." He didn't sound bitter, just resolved to the fact the military would never be able to do its job adequately with the current state of government interference.

"You mentioned the other night about possibly leaving the DEA. Were you serious?"

"Absolutely. I'll finish my open cases, testify at the upcoming trial, then figure out my next move." He set her foot down and picked up the other, using his thumbs to make slow, deep circles on the bottom.

"I'm sure Heath would welcome you here. He and Jace are always looking for good men."

He continued holding her foot in one hand while the other moved under her jeans to massage her calf. She moaned at the feel of his hand on her skin.

"Staying here would complicate things, Brooke."

"Explain to me why. I don't understand the reason we can't be together. We're both single, and it's obvious we both have feelings for each other. You don't make any sense." She pulled her leg free and sat up, resting her arms across her bent knees. "Help me understand."

"I don't know if I can. Our lives, backgrounds, couldn't be more different."

"Why does the past matter? Isn't it who we are now and not our past that matters?"

"The past shapes us, Brooke. No matter how much you want to deny it, I just don't fit in the life you grew up in—a regular home, two parents, brothers, plenty of food, and clothes. I had none of those."

She reached forward and grabbed his hands in hers. "What did you have?"

He sighed, not wanting to delve into his past. He looked down at their joined hands. It felt so right, her touch so perfect, he didn't want to let go and yet, he knew the odds were slim they could ever have more than this.

"We were poor...dirt poor. My mother worked two jobs to make enough for food, clothes, and rent, and still there were times we went to bed hungry. I didn't have new clothes until I went into the Army, never a new shirt, pants or shoes. Nothing. I started working after school when I was ten at a small grocery store then worked at the ranch when I turned fifteen. Somehow we made it."

"That's what this is all about? You grew up poor?" Her hands stilled on his as her face began to redden. "How could you ever believe coming from a family with no money would matter to me?"

Kade stood, his jaw working as his eyes narrowed. "My mother wasn't married. I never had a father, never even met the man."

She glared at him, not giving an inch. "Fine. So you're a bastard. I'm sure you've been called worse."

His eyes locked on hers. He didn't break the stare even as his lips twitched a moment before he burst into laughter. "God, Brooke. You are something." He moved forward, wrapped his arms around her, pulling her close.

She tightened her arms around him and buried her head on his chest, breathing in his unique scent and wanting to stay this way forever. She looked up as he lowered his head to brush his lips across hers before covering her mouth in a hungry kiss, sending spirals of pleasure through her.

He broke the kiss, letting his lips sear a path down the soft column of her neck to her shoulder. She let her head fall back with a moan as he continued the wonderful torture. He eased his way up, along the curve of her jaw, before nibbling at her earlobe.

"We just keep catching you two like this." Paige's voice had them pushing apart. She stood outside the tent, Nesto beside her.

Kade cleared his throat, took another look at Brooke and placed one more kiss on her lips before grabbing his hat. "Goodnight, ladies. I'll see you in the morning." He stepped outside and sent a warning look at his friend as he started across the campsite. "Don't say a word." Kade's voice was more of a growl than request.

Nesto's hand clasped his shoulder. "Come on, man. You might as well give in to it. Why fight your feelings?" They walked toward the tent they shared with Blake, stopping a few feet away.

"Because she's too good for me and you know it." The defeat in Kade's voice cut through Nesto.

"Why don't you let Brooke be the judge of that?"

******

"How'd it go?" Heath asked as Cam took a seat in the study next to Jace. He'd returned home the night before after presenting the purchase offer to Ty, Chris, and Rafe.

"Good, although they were non-committal. They need a chance to review everything in detail."

"Did Rafe raise any questions about the corporation making the offer?"

"Not yet. It will come up at some point, I'm sure, so we need to be prepared." He glanced from Heath to Jace.

"The two of you need to figure how you'll deal with it when he learns who's behind the offer."

Neither responded, knowing the entire purchase hinged on Rafe's reaction.

"Any indication about when they'll get back to you?" Jace asked.

"Chris and Ty are anxious. I suspect they'll have a few requests but no deal breakers. Rafe is a wild card. He does not want to sell. He loves the business." Cam pursed his lips, knowing he had to bring up the next subject even though it made him uncomfortable. "Ty told me Rafe and his wife are finalizing a divorce. It's the first time anyone mentioned it. He spends most of his time at the business, even bunking down there several nights a week when he's in town."

"If his personal life's falling apart, he's more apt to focus on his business and won't want to give it up." Jace leaned forward, resting his arms on his knees.

"What about his sons" Heath asked.

"According to Chris and Ty, they are a real asset to the business. I don't know how they're dealing with the issues between Rafe and their mother. It never came up." Cam stood and stretched, then walked over to the wall of family pictures, focusing on the one with the three brothers, standing shoulder to shoulder, holding the reins to their horses, and sporting wide grins. He turned back to Heath and Jace, knowing they were in a tough situation.

"Nothing we can do now except wait." Heath stopped as his phone rang. "Hey, Trey. What's going on?" He listened, not interrupting. "You know it's no problem. When will you get here?" He looked at his calendar, knowing any day they arrived would be fine. "Keep Annie and me posted. We'll see you next Friday."

"Trey, huh?"

"He and Jesse are both being deployed. Trey for a short period, Jesse for longer. Ryan and Paul, also." Heath glanced at Jace then Cam. "Odd they'd all be called up at once. Must be some type of major maneuver or something. Anyway, they aren't sure yet how long Jesse will be gone. They're bringing Trevor to stay with us."

"A trip back to parenthood." Jace grinned at Heath. He and Caroline still had one boy at home. Hopefully it would be several years before grandkids came along.

"Sounds like it. I'd better tell Annie."

"You know, Lainey would love to help with him. Trevor could come to Colorado and stay with us for a while, and attend Lainey's preschool. It's an option to consider if you want." Cam's wife, Lainey, ran a prosperous preschool in Fire Mountain, and had opened another one in Cold Creek, Colorado, near the company the MacLarens bought several months before.

"Thanks, Cam. We might do that depending on how long he'll be here. Let us know the moment you hear anything from Chris or Ty."

"Will do," Cam said as he followed Heath and Jace toward the kitchen to tell Annie the news.

Chapter Fourteen

Brooke collapsed on her bed roll, exhausted from Saturday's long ride, yet feeling a wonderful sense of exhilaration. She stretched, feeling every muscle, including a few she forgot she had.

"What a great ride," Paige said in an excited, but tired voice as she entered the tent and sat on her bed roll. "Don't you think so?"

"I haven't been over such beautiful, rocky terrain since my mother married Heath and I started riding again." She sat up and stretched her arms above her head. "You seemed to spend a lot of time with Nesto. How are the two of you doing?"

Paige smiled. "We're doing well. He asked if he can call me when I get back to San Diego. I said yes, of course."

"He's a very nice man."

"Yes, he is. As is Kade." Paige knew her friend struggled with her feelings toward him, even though it couldn't have been more obvious how they felt about each other.

"I'd better help Cassie with supper." Brooke stood and walked outside.

"I'll come with you."

Cassie had already pulled out the chicken enchilada casseroles and begun to warm them in the special camp ovens the family assembled years before. Blake helped tend the fires while Kade and Nesto took care of inspecting the tack and saddles for the ride tomorrow.

"How can we help?" Brooke asked, spotting Kade near the trailers with his unbuttoned shirt pulled from his jeans, flapping in the evening breeze. Her breath caught at the sight he made, a sprinkling of crisp hair over taut chest muscles. She wanted to run her hands over him, feel his warm skin beneath hers.

"You can grab the tortillas and set them near the stove." Cassie's voice broke through the fantasy Brooke had begun to weave. "The plates and utensils are in the plastic box next to the cooler, and the brownies are inside."

Brooke and Paige did as Cassie asked, finishing as the others began to emerge from their tents and mill about the tables.

Tonight, Kade took a seat next to Brooke. They'd spoken little during the ride, not even when they'd stopped for lunch.

Tonight she noticed the warmth radiating from his body and shifted a little closer, allowing their thighs to touch. Out of the corner of her eye she saw him set down his fork and lower his hand below the table. He rested it on her thigh and squeezed, just enough to send a bolt of heat through her body. She could feel her face warm as she drew in a breath. He looked over and she noticed his eyes crinkle at the corners as his mouth tipped up. The man was a tease.

"If everyone is finished, I'd like to review our ride for tomorrow. It won't be as long since we'll need to be back here by midafternoon to pack and head out." Cassie set down her notebook before explaining the destination, what they'd see, and safety precautions. After a few questions, everyone dispersed.

Kade squeezed Brooke's thigh once more and leaned toward her. "Let's take a walk after everything's cleaned up." He didn't wait for a reply. He stood, grabbed both of their plates and walked toward the wash basin, while Brooke helped Cassie and Paige clear away extra food. They'd just finished when she saw Kade step next to her.

"You ready?"

Brooke glanced at the others, seeing Paige and Nesto both hiding smiles, and wondered if Kade had said something to let Nesto know they had become an item. Or had they? His actions seemed much different than his words, which confused her, prompting a cautious approach until she understood his true intentions. Did he want to be friends or had he decided he wanted more? She suspected he already knew what she wanted.

"Yes. Let's go." She wiped her hands on a towel, then let him guide her to a path behind the horse trailers which led to a rocky outcropping.

Kade took the lead, holding out his hand to help her over the taller rocks. They didn't speak on their way to the top, not even when they stopped for a moment to watch the sun slip behind the mountains. He took her hand and they covered the last few yards with ease, ending on a flat rock shelf facing east. Brooke walked to the edge, Kade behind her, and she felt his arms wrap around her waist and pull her against his chest.

"It's beautiful." Brooke let her head fall back and took a deep breath.

He nuzzled her neck with his lips, placing soft kisses behind her ear. "I know."

They stayed rooted in place until the lack of light would hinder their descent if they didn't start back.

"We'd better get going." Kade's reluctant tone mirrored Brooke's feelings.

They hiked down the hillside toward camp, again keeping their thoughts to themselves until they'd walked past the campfire where most everyone else sat roasting marshmallows. Kade tugged her behind a tent and wrapped his arms around her.

"I don't know what I'm doing around you. If you knew everything, you'd change your mind about me." His somber gaze emphasized his deep belief in his words.

"Tell me what it is. How can either of us know how I'll react unless I understand what stands between us."

He looked down at her and brushed his lips against hers as he spoke. "All right, but not tonight. After Nesto leaves for San Diego we'll talk and I'll tell you everything. Then you can decide."

****

Nesto's last week passed faster than he anticipated. He and Paige spent considerable time together, almost every free minute when he and Kade weren't tending horses or helping the MacLarens with other work. She had another month before she'd be returning to San Diego. They both agreed it would give them each time to decide how much more they expected from a relationship. He wanted it all—she took a more cautious approach. Regardless, they'd committed to seeing each other once she got back to San Diego.

"You ready to head out?" Kade asked as they stood next to Nesto's truck. His friend had spent a couple of hours with Paige the previous night saying goodbye.

"Yep. I'd like to miss the Friday afternoon traffic heading into San Diego. Besides," he turned and glanced in the direction of Brooke's cabin where Paige would still be sleeping. "I need to clear my head."

"I hear ya, man," Kade said and clasped his shoulder.

"You *will* be coming back when your leaves ends, right, bro?"

"Yes. I'll be back." Kade knew he'd return to his job for a while, until he decided his next move. He still had two open cases requiring his testimony, if they made it to trial.

Kade watched as Nesto drove down the road toward the highway. It had been a good two weeks. They hadn't spent such a long stretch together, talking and catching up, in a long time. A few drinks a couple times a week didn't cut it after a lifetime of friendship. He jumped in his truck and started for the ranch. He had work to do. Heath had told him Trey and his family would be flying in late in the afternoon and asked Kade to make sure their horses were ready for a Saturday ride. He was glad for the distraction. It kept his mind off Brooke.

******

Cam poked his head into Heath's office. "You have a minute?"

"Sure do." Heath pushed aside the document he'd been reviewing, thankful for a break from the tedious agreement.

"I heard from Chris at RTC. He and Ty put together a list of requested modifications. Here it is."

Cam slid a copy across the desk and waited while Heath read through it.

"None of these are deal killers."

"Rafe refused to give his thoughts. Chris said he's pretty angry about the whole situation, even though the offer requests he stay on as president with a substantial increase in pay. He and Ty believe Rafe never thought it would go this far. Anyway, he took off yesterday and they can't find him."

"Did Chris give any indication Rafe discovered who would be buying the company?" Heath asked.

"No. He said it never came up."

Heath nodded and glanced down at the list once more. "I'll get in touch with the others, run the requests by them, and ask Colt to prepare an updated offer."

"And Rafe?" Cam asked.

"It only takes two to agree to the sale—Chris and Ty. We'll deal with Rafe if the sale goes through."

Cam stood and walked toward the door.

"Cam? Don't forget Trey's coming in tonight. Supper tomorrow at our place."

"We'll be here."

Heath leaned back in his chair, thinking of Rafe and his reaction to the sale. They'd set a course of action and they had to stick to it, even knowing there would be a confrontation at some point. He and Jace planned to fly to Crooked Tree as soon as the deal finalized, meet with Rafe, and hope some type of compromise could be reached—both for the business and for the family.

******

"They're here," Annie called as she walked outside to greet Trey, Jesse, and Trevor, picking up her grandson when he ran toward her. "How was the trip?"

"Easy, as always." Trey, then Jesse, gave her a hug and followed her inside.

Cassie, Brooke, and Eric were already waiting. The rest of the family and a few friends would be there tomorrow night for supper. Tonight, Trey asked it be kept small.

The supper conversation centered on the orders Jesse, Trey, and the others had received. Lots of questions with few answers.

"I wish I could tell you more. We've all been activated, which is odd, but not unheard of. I don't know how long Trevor will need to stay." Trey sipped his wine and held Jesse's hand.

"Trevor will be fine with us for as long as you need. Don't worry about it." Heath took another bite of pie, then set down his fork. "The problem is, Annie may not want to give him back."

Trey looked at his stepmom and chuckled. "That's what Jesse said."

"When do you fly out?" Eric asked.

"First of the week," Trey said. "I'm sorry to end this so early, but I'm beat." He stood and pulled out Jesse's chair. "We'll see you in the morning."

"Trail ride tomorrow, if you're up for it." Eric stood to leave.

"Sounds great. We could use some downtime."

"Guess I'll be leaving, too," Brooke said as she grabbed her keys and purse. "Paige and I will be here early." She walked out to her car and drove toward her cabin. She could see the lights on in Kade's place and thought for a moment of turning the wheel instead of heading straight home. They'd spoken little since their return from the weekend trip. He'd kept busy all week, almost as if he meant to avoid her. He'd never been rude, just hadn't gone out of his way to see her.

Brooke came to the turn and stopped. Left toward her place or right toward his. She sat a moment, weighing the merits of one over the other. She turned left.

"Hey. You're back early." Paige finished rinsing her plate and set it on the counter. "Did you have a good time?"

"It's always good to see them. We're set for a ride tomorrow morning and supper with everyone tomorrow night." She tossed her keys on a table and plopped onto the sofa. "Did you speak with Nesto?"

"Yeah. He called right after you left."

Brooke didn't respond, slumping further into the sofa.

"Why don't you drive over and see him?" Paige asked.

Brooke's head swung to Paige. "You know why. He's barely spoken to me all week, and has gone out of his way to avoid me sometimes. It's as if last weekend never happened."

Paige sat next to her. "Go. You know you want to and nothing will get resolved until you get it all out in the open." Paige leaned back in the sofa, resting a book in her lap.

"He could slam the door in my face."

"He won't."

******

Kade paced the living room, walking between the sofa, fireplace, and front window, holding a glass of ice water in his hand. He'd just finished five hundred sit-ups and a hundred push-ups, trying to purge Brooke from his mind. It had been a wasted effort. He stopped and gazed outside, taking a long swallow of water, hoping it would cool him off.

For the last hour, he'd thought of nothing except calling Brooke. He'd followed a schedule all week to keep himself too busy to spend time with her. She hadn't approached him or said anything, even when he'd caught her staring at him, confusion on her face. The time had come to tell her everything or let her go. He walked to the counter, then turned at the sound of a car engine.

Brooke cut the engine and stared at Kade's cabin. The lights were on, his truck and motorcycle were in the carport, and her heart pounded in a bold staccato. She pulled the key from the ignition, opened the door, and stepped outside, taking a deep breath and forcing her legs to move forward.

She stopped a few inches from the front door. Brooke raised a hand to knock, then wiped her damp hands down her jeans. She swallowed the lump in her throat, took a steadying breath, and tapped on his door.

Kade knew who stood outside, he could feel it. He set down his drink, covered the short distance across the room in a few long strides, and pulled the door open. His eyes wandered over her. She wore jeans, yellow top, and sandals, and was the most beautiful woman he'd ever seen.

"I...uh, hope I'm not—"

He reached out, grabbed her hand, and pulled her inside, kicking the door closed, before pushing her against it and covering her mouth with his.

Brooke's initial apprehension gave way to an all-consuming desire. She wrapped her arms around his neck, enjoying the feel of his hard body aligned with hers, his mouth hot and searching. She felt his hands grab hers, pulling them from around his neck and raising them above her head as his lips broke contact with her mouth to move down her neck to her shoulder.

His warm, moist lips set her aflame. He moved up to her mouth, exploring it thoroughly before pulling back, dropping her hands, and resting his forehead against hers.

"Make love to me, Kade," Brooke whispered as her eyes locked with his.

"Brooke, you don't know—"

She didn't let him finish, pulling him back down, her mouth devouring his.

Blood thrummed in Kade's temples as he felt the heat of her burning through him.

"Please, Kade…"

He swept her into his arms, his mouth fused to hers, and walked the few feet to his bedroom, kicking the door open before stopping at the edge of the bed. He lowered her gently and followed her down, aligning his body alongside hers. He rested a hand on her stomach, staring down at her with heated eyes.

"Are you sure?" Kade asked, his voice husky with desire.

She reached up and clasped her hands behind his head, drawing him down, "Yes, quite sure."

Chapter Fifteen

Brooke stretched, arching her body in a lazy movement, causing Kade's blood to heat all over again. They'd made love until the early morning, fell asleep, then woke up to make love once more. Still, he wanted her again and ran his knuckles down her cheek, then fingered strands of her long blonde hair. He bent down and pressed his lips to hers, inhaling the coconut vanilla scent he'd come to recognize as hers.

Her eyes, feeling heavy, fluttered open. "Good morning."

"Good morning, beautiful."

"Hmmm...I feel good." Her voice purred and was met by a soft chuckle from Kade.

"I'd hope so." A crooked smile twisted his lips. He bent and took her mouth with his again before pulling back and sliding out of bed. "I'm starving." He grabbed his jeans, slipped into them, then turned back toward the bed, throwing his t-shirt at her. "Come on. You can help."

Brooke watched him walk from the room, admiring his powerful body and the way his jeans hugged every delicious curve. She thought it odd how comfortable she felt waking up in his bed, Kade beside her, his eyes filled with desire. She stood, pulled on his t-shirt, splashed water on her face before dragging a brush through her hair, and followed him to the kitchen, already smelling the enticing scent of fresh-brewed coffee.

"Here you go." He handed her a cup filled with coffee and pointed to the cream and sugar. She breathed in the aroma, then took a sip.

"Mmm. This is good." Brooke flashed him a dazzling smile.

"You sound surprised. I'll have you know I'm considered a damn fine cook."

"By whom?"

He fell silent, his sheepish expression told all she needed to know about who had found his cooking so fabulous in the past.

"Well, there's a new sheriff in town and it appears you'll have to prove yourself all over again."

"Sheriff, huh?" Amusement flickered in his eyes.

She met his gaze, not responding as she continued to sip her hot coffee. "What can I do to help?"

Kade set some fruit on the counter with a cutting board and knife. "Have at it." He turned back to the bacon and eggs, and once again Brooke felt her face heat at the sight he made.

She'd just finished cutting the fruit and scooping it into a bowl when he piled the hot food on two plates and walked to the dining table.

"More coffee?" he asked.

"Not yet." She eyed breakfast, her mouth watering, and placed hand over her stomach at the spontaneous growl.

Kade laughed. "Guess the food came just in time."

They dug in without another word, both ravenous after their night of passion. It wasn't long before Kade took his last bite and pushed his plate away. Brooke finished a couple of minutes later, sipping her coffee and leaning forward.

"Is now a good time for you to tell me everything about why we can't be together?"

The relaxed humor she'd seen in his face a few moments before disappeared, replaced by a look of resignation. He pushed back his chair and stood, shoving his hands in his pockets and walking toward the front window, his back to her.

"Are you certain you want to know? Once it's out, there will be no taking it back." His voice had turned hard and apprehensive.

She walked up behind him and wrapped her arms around his waist, resting her head against his back. "Don't you think it's time I know what's tearing you apart?" She could feel his chest expand and contract as he took a deep breath.

He turned toward Brooke, pulling her to him. "Yes, it's time. Let's sit down." They walked to the sofa when both of their phones started to ring. "I guess we'd better answer."

Brooke glanced at caller ID. "Hi, Paige. What's up?"

"Where are you two? Everyone is waiting." Paige paused a moment, realizing Brooke had no idea what she referred to. "The ride, remember? Your family, horses, picnic?"

"Oh my God." She looked to Kade who'd just hung up his call. "The ride."

"I know. That was Heath. Let's get out of here."

She dashed to his room, dressed, then grabbed her boots, hat, and gloves from her car and threw them into Kade's truck. He tore down the dirt road toward the main house.

"Are you all right?" he asked when he noticed her biting her lower lip and gripping her hands tight in her lap.

She looked at him then back at the road. "Sure. Fine."

"It'll be okay." He reached over and placed a hand on her arm. "Stick with me."

Brooke wasn't sure what he meant, but nodded as they pulled to a stop next to the barn and jumped from the truck.

As Paige had said, everyone stood around, horses ready, waiting for her and Kade. Brooke did her best to ignore the knowing glances as she felt heat creep up her neck. She turned at the sound of Kade's voice.

"My apologies, Heath. I blew it. None of this is Brooke's fault."

Heath looked between Kade and Brooke, his face impassive. "You're here now. Let's get going."

A bit of good natured ribbing occurred for the first few miles. To Brooke's surprise, no one seemed shocked at seeing her and Kade drive up together.

"How are you doing?"

Brooke looked over to see Kade reined in alongside her. He'd been riding near the front with Eric, Trey, and Cam, and she could hear their laughter echo to the back where she rode with Paige and Cassie.

"Good. A little sore." She cast him a teasing smile and got one from him in return.

"No doubt." He fell silent a moment, as if deciding what to say. "How do you feel about coming over after supper tonight? We still need to have our talk."

"As I recall, I believe it's you who'll be doing most of the talking."

"You're right. Afterwards, once I've explained everything, we can talk about a future—if we have one."

She looked over at him and nodded, her sense of happiness fading at his words. Perhaps her expectations after their night together were more unrealistic than she thought. Well, she was a big girl. Whatever happened, she'd deal with it as she had everything else.

"By the way. You should know Eric, Cam, and Trey came over to my place last night. They saw your car, noticed the lights were out, and didn't stop."

He smiled at the groan she made.

"Nothing we can do about it now. Guess I'll check with Heath, see if he needs me to ride point." Kade tapped his heel into the horse he rode today, a beautiful bay gelding with black mane, tail, and lower legs. Picasso had belonged to Brooke's father, Kit, and her mother had never been able to part with him. She had to admit the horse and rider made a stunning pair.

"What was that about?" Paige asked as she and Cassie rode up on either side.

"He wants me to come over after supper tonight so we can talk."

"Talk?" Cassie asked.

"He wants to clear the air, explain some things to me." She glanced over at Cassie and shrugged. "Whatever happens...happens."

******

"Are you ready, Paige?" Brooke had finished her shower, dressed, and was sorting through the mail she'd received at the main house. Nothing too exciting, with one exception. A letter came from the university, officially congratulating her on obtaining her degree and Ph.D. designation.

"All set." Paige grabbed a lightweight jacket and headed for the front door. "Is there anything we need to take?"

"Nope. Mom has it covered."

They climbed into Brooke's car, driving past Kade's cabin. His truck still sat out front but the chopper was gone. She pulled to a stop in front of the ranch house and climbed out, noticing both Eric's and Kade's motorcycles parked together. She'd heard the guys talk when they stopped for lunch today, encouraging Cam and Trey to get bikes so they could all ride. The conversation surprised her given the fact Trey couldn't visit often and Kade would be leaving in a few weeks. She ignored the gripping pain slicing through her at the thought.

They walked through the front door and were immediately assaulted with the noise level from having all the MacLarens and Sinclairs in one place. No matter how uncertain her future with Kade, she knew she'd always be able to count on her family.

"Brooke, Paige, come on into the kitchen and I'll put you to work." Annie smiled at them as she set down a tray loaded with chips, salsa, and guacamole.

They greeted everyone as each grabbed a drink and walked into the kitchen. Brooke noticed Kade speaking with Jace, and smiled at him when he glanced her way, receiving a brief nod in return. Her stomach sank. Something seemed off and she began to prepare herself for a night of disappointment.

"Brooke, please take the potatoes to the table. Paige, you can grab the bowls of vegetables. The salads are just about ready."

"Where are Heath and Cam?" Brooke asked her mom.

"Out back manning the barbeque. They insisted on steaks and ribs, so I told them they were in charge of the meat."

They turned at the sound of the men coming in from the back.

"Here you are, ladies. Three plates of meat as ordered," Cam said as they walked toward the large dining table.

"I guess we're ready. Brooke, do you and Paige want to get everyone to the table?"

"Sure, Mom. I doubt it will take much persuading with this group."

Within minutes everyone took seats. Brooke held a place for Kade, hoping he'd decide to join her. She looked behind her to see him walk in from the patio with Eric, each holding a beer. To her relief, he broke away and came toward her.

"Did you save this seat for me?"

"I did, unless you've got a better offer."

He sat down, leaned over, and placed a kiss on her cheek. "Never." His gaze held hers for a moment, causing her heart to trip.

His response was what Brooke needed to relieve the tension she'd been feeling all day. She needed to relax, enjoy the evening, and not jump to conclusions.

"All right, everyone." Heath stood at the end of the table, holding a glass in his hand. "Here's to Trey and Jesse, and our extended family back on the base. We don't know where they're headed, but they'll carry our prayers and wishes for a safe journey with them."

The room quieted before Trey spoke up. "Hey, this is a celebration of getting us all together. Come on. Let's eat." He speared a thick steak and planted it on his plate.

"How much longer will you be at the ranch, Kade?" Jesse asked from across the table.

"I have another six weeks of leave, then I'll head back." He glanced at Brooke, a grim smile on his face.

"Have they given you any idea what you'll be doing next?" Trey asked.

"Matter of fact, I got a call this afternoon. There's a new task force being established and my name came up in the conversation. They're still working out the details, but it looks like I may be doing some major traveling."

"Undercover?" Cam jumped in.

"That's what I do. Undercover, long days and even longer nights." He picked up his beer and took a long swallow. He couldn't tell them he didn't want this assignment, not yet. He was growing tired of the dangerous assignments and the long nights working undercover, but until he decided on his next step, it was all he had.

The conversation turned to other topics—Cam and Lainey's new home in Cold Creek, the trip Jace and Caroline planned to take, Blake returning to school, and Cassie's final year of college. Kade was glad to have the conversation turn away from him.

He'd noticed the look on Brooke's face change from joy to confusion as he answered each question. They had to get through supper and head over to his place. She needed to know about his plans for the future. Most of all, she needed to learn about his past. Her response would tell him whether they had any chance at all or if a future with her was as remote as he'd always thought.

Brooke tried to breath. She felt like a fist had landed a hard blow to her stomach and pushed all the air from her lungs. He'd said he wanted out, had been looking at alternatives to the DEA, possibly talking to Heath and Jace about a position at the ranch. His answers to the questions tonight made it clear he'd made the decision to return to San Diego and his position as an undercover agent, working day and night, on the most dangerous assignments.

She placed a hand on her stomach to quell the knot twisting inside. She knew her feelings for Kade were real. She'd never felt anything so strong, compelling, and all-consuming for another person. She loved him.

Brooke didn't know the extent of Kade's feelings for her, except every fiber of her being believed he cared a great deal. He may not love her, but she meant something to him—she'd stake her life on it—yet he'd said nothing about his change of plans.

Kade had tried to tell her something important that morning. Had it only been fourteen hours since they'd been together in bed, making love, and feeling as if nothing could come between them?

She felt his hand touch hers, and looked to see him entwine their fingers as he leaned close to her ear.

"Relax. We'll talk tonight."

"Will I like what I hear?"

He narrowed his gaze. "I doubt it, but you need to know." He took a breath. "It may be a deal breaker for us, Brooke."

She couldn't imagine anything he could tell her that would change her feelings. Unless, of course, he had a wife, but she already knew that wasn't the case. Brooke ran through all the possibilities she could conjure up— nothing came close to being bad enough to make her walk. She knew his years in Special Ops and the DEA had worn on him. At the same time, those experiences had molded him into the man she loved. Nothing he could tell her from those parts of his life would change a thing.

How would she react if he told her he'd decided to stay with the DEA? Could they make it work with her in Arizona and him on assignment in locations he couldn't divulge? Brooke wanted to believe they could.

She knew Cam and Lainey sometimes spent a couple of weeks apart due to his traveling. Trey and Jesse spent months apart as Navy pilots tasked to different groups. Brooke would also be traveling with her new job. Yes, she could handle it with Kade if that's what it took for a relationship to work.

As her mind tried to identify what he might say, she began to relax. Nothing he could tell her would alter how she felt. Nothing.

"Any word from Montana?" Trey asked his father.

Her stepbrother's voice broke the pattern of her thoughts and she looked at Trey.

"Not unless Cam's heard something since yesterday." Heath glanced at his stepson.

"Colt drew up the changes and I sent them to Chris and Ty yesterday. I doubt we'll hear anything until midweek." Cam leaned back and slipped an arm around Lainey as the sound of pounding on the front door caused everyone's gaze to shift toward the entry.

"I'll get it." Eric walked to the door as the pounding started again and pulled it open. He didn't recognize the man in front of him. "Are you looking for someone?"

"Damn straight I am." He pushed passed Eric and stalked toward the dining room, glanced around the table, looking for one specific person. He stopped and stared, locking eyes with the man he sought. He crossed his arms and planted his feet shoulder width apart, his nostrils flaring as anger coursed through him. "What the hell do you think you're doing?" he barked out.

Heath stood, never taking his eyes off the man.

"Hello, Rafe. It's good to see you."

Chapter Sixteen

No one moved or said a word as the two faced off, except for Jace. He stood and walked around the table, stopping a foot away.

"Can I get you something to drink?"

Rafe broke eye contact with Heath long enough to glance at his younger brother. "Whiskey. Make it a double."

Jace walked toward the bar, poured the drink for Rafe, and handed him the glass. His brother tossed it down in one quick move, then set the glass on a nearby table. He looked around the room, recognizing Cam and Eric, but no one else.

"Family gathering?" he asked in a sarcastic tone, his question directed at Heath.

"They're a part of your family, too, Rafe."

"Like hell they are." He made no attempt to move closer to his older brother as he scanned the room, noting little had changed over the years other than some new furniture and an updated kitchen. "It looks the same."

"It worked for you, Jace, and me growing up. I saw no reason to change it." Heath picked up his glass of wine and took a sip as Annie stood up and whispered in his ear. He nodded and looked back at Rafe. "I suspect you're here to talk about the offer. We can go into the study if you want to discuss this in private."

"They can stay. It's going to be a short talk. I'm not here to negotiate. I want you to rescind your offer."

"Not going to happen." Heath focused on Rafe and waited.

"Why not? Don't you have enough? Is it ever enough for you?" Rafe asked.

"This isn't a matter of expanding just to acquire more companies. You've built a good business, it fits our needs, and expands what we have. Besides, it's a damn fine offer. You'll get a large percentage of ownership, stay on as president, your sons stay on, plus you obtain your share of the other MacLaren properties. Hell, Rafe, it's the best offer you'll ever get." Heath set down his wine glass, walked to the bar and poured a shot of whiskey.

"They contacted you, didn't they?"

"Yes. Chris and Ty sent an inquiry."

Cam glanced at Heath, Jace, then at Rafe. He tried to put himself in Rafe's place and found he could understand how the man felt. Betrayed, backed into a corner with little room to maneuver. He'd feel the same if it were him, but he hoped he'd also be able to see the benefits of what Heath and Jace offered. It would be a boon to Rafe and his family, and it would allow him a good measure of autonomy.

"They had no right to go behind my back."

"They knew we'd offer a fair price and terms. If we don't buy it, someone else will, and I can guarantee you won't get anywhere close to the deal sitting on the table right now." Heath took a step closer, noting his brother had aged well. He wasn't much younger than Heath, with smooth olive skin, and bright green eyes.

"What's the real reason you're going after this so hard, offering such a sweet deal?"

"Two reasons. First, as I said, it's a good move for us. Second, we want you back in the family. It's been too long." He walked to within a couple of feet from Rafe, never letting his eyes drop from his brother's. "Take it Rafe. We want you back with us."

"No. Not this way, when you know it's not what I want. You're just like father, manipulating people until you get what you want. But you won't do it to me. I'm not a true part of this family and never will be." His voice had risen with each word as a slight red tinge began to creep up his neck.

"Just take the damn offer. It's over. Accept it and move on." The deep, unyielding voice, coming from someone no one expected would speak, was hard, emphatic. He stood, turned from the others and started to leave the room in slow, measured strides.

Cam straightened in his seat, as did the others around the table and stared at the person who'd thrown out the challenge. Stunned, Eric began to stand and walk over to him before Heath gestured with his hand to stay put.

Rafe rounded on the man who'd dared to interfere and took several steps toward his retreating back. "Who the hell are you to tell me what I should be doing?"

The man turned, arms slack at his side, and locked eyes with a man he knew, but didn't.

"My full name is Kade Santiago Taylor MacLaren. Reyna Santiago is my mother. You're my father." Kade heard the gasp and shifted his gaze to see Brooke put a hand over her mouth, disbelief showing in her eyes, taking a step backward as if wanting to flee the room. He didn't blame her. It's what he'd expected.

His eyes made a quick scan of those present, noting the look of surprise, mixed with confusion, on everyone's face. Except Heath and Jace. Had they known?

"Reyna? You're Reyna's son?" Rafe's shaky voice cracked.

"I'm Reyna's and your son. I'm the boy you walked away from years ago." The vehemence in his tone surprised even him. All the anger he'd felt at being abandoned, not wanted, surged forth. He had to get out of there before he did something he'd regret. Kade turned and walked from the room, slamming the door behind him. A minute later, the roar of a chopper firing up signaled he'd taken off.

Rafe staggered backwards and collapsed into a chair, scrubbing a hand over his face, stunned at the turn of events.

Annie walked toward Brooke and put an arm around her. "Come on, honey. We'll let the brothers work this out." She glanced around, encouraging the others to follow. One by one they left, retreating toward the large family room in the back of the house.

228

Trey walked over to his father. "Is it true?"

"Yes. Kade is Rafe's son," Heath answered. "I'll tell all of you about it once we talk with Rafe."

Trey took another look at Rafe, the uncle he'd never met, and left to join the others. He wanted to find Kade, make sure he was all right, but thought better of it. He'd speak with him tomorrow, before he and Jesse flew to California. He wanted to welcome him into the family—let him know they were glad to have him as part of the MacLarens.

******

"I need to find him, Mom." Brooke started to leave, wanting him to know none of this mattered. She'd seen the anger in his eyes when they'd locked on hers. There'd been no time to go to him before he stormed from the house.

"You may want to give him some time. Let his anger settle a little, and give yourself time to decide what you want." Annie grabbed her daughter's hands and squeezed.

"I want him. None of this matters to me."

"And his job?" Annie asked.

"He said he wants to make a change." She squeezed her eyes shut then opened them to look at her mother. "He asked to talk with me after supper, explain his past and talk about his job. I guess this is what he planned to tell me."

Annie noticed Trey walk up beside her. "We're going to put Trevor to bed. As soon as he's settled, Jesse and I will be back down."

"Since it appears no one is planning to leave, we might as well get comfortable." Everyone chose a seat in the large family room and prepared for long stay. Annie and Brooke looked across the room at Eric who held up three movies. "Here are the choices."

"Where are the chick flicks?" Paige asked.

"Not part of the deal tonight. Okay, Lord of the Rings, Expendables, or Red?"

"Red?" Lainey asked.

Cam looked at his wife. "Are you kidding me? It's a great film. You know, Bruce Willis, Morgan Freeman, John Malkovich, and a few others you'd know." He looked at Eric. "I vote for Red."

"Same here," Trey said as he left the room with Trevor.

Cassie elbowed her cousins, Blake and Brett.

"Yeah, that's good with us," Blake muttered. He and his brother were already immersed in games on their cell phones. A movie would be background noise to them.

"I guess I'll make coffee and bring in dessert. It may be a long night."

Brooke watched as Annie left, feeling conflicted. She wanted to go to Kade, be there for him. Her heart ached at the pain she saw on his face when he'd informed Rafe of their relationship. No matter how old someone got, what life had thrown at them, or how strong they'd become, the hurt of being abandoned by a parent never quite went away.

"Brooke, come over and sit with us," Paige said and patted a spot between her and Lainey.

She'd stay for a while, give Kade some space, then go search for him. No way would she let him be alone tonight.

******

"Here. Drink these." Heath held out a shot glass of whiskey and a hot cup of coffee.

Rafe looked up, took the whiskey and shot it down before reaching for the coffee. He took a couple of sips, letting the hot liquid burn his mouth and throat. For whatever reason, the pain felt right.

Heath sat in a chair next to him while Jace leaned against a nearby cabinet.

"What a mess." Rafe's voice sounded tired, broken. He leaned back in his chair and closed his eyes. "What the boy said is true. There isn't a doubt in my mind I'm his father." He looked over at Heath. "Did you and Jace know?"

"Kade never said a word. When he was in the house, he'd sometimes wander into the study where the picture of the three of us from high school is hanging on the wall. I caught him staring at it a few times and got suspicious."

"You hired someone to check him out?"

"Jace and I talked about it. Decided it was the right thing to do. You know he was in Army Special Forces before joining the DEA as an agent. Kade's got quite a record. Earned his bachelor's degree while in the service. No help from anyone—all on his own."

Rafe cleared his throat. "And Reyna?"

"She moved after he graduated from high school. We didn't learn where. Kade took a leave from the DEA after his last assignment. My stepdaughter, Brooke, told me he'd worked horses during high school. I asked him to come here, work the horses for us, help my daughter Cassie with her riding students. He jumped on it. Of course, Jace and I already knew who he was by then. Still, he never said a word to either of us. I doubt he ever would have until you showed up tonight. You ought to be real proud of him, Rafe."

Rafe swallowed hard. He looked at Heath, then Jace. "I loved her—his mother, Reyna. Asked her to marry me, more than once, but she always refused. This was before..." his voice trailed off. "Anyway, she disappeared one night. She and her family just vanished from Crooked Tree. I checked with everyone, but no one knew where they'd gone. Time passed, and when she didn't return, I moved on. Met my wife." He rubbed his eyes and looked at the floor. "I'd been seeing Deidre for about a year. Just asked her to marry me. We were at a small diner, ready to leave, when I saw Reyna and a young boy sitting in a booth. She looked at me with the big brown eyes that always drew me to her, and glanced at the boy. He looked up and stared right at me. God, he looked just like me—eyes, hair, face. I knew right then, but I did nothing. *Nothing.* She'd turned me down so many times, then disappeared...Hell. That's just an excuse." He pinched the bridge of his nose between his thumb and forefinger. "She didn't approach me, probably because I was with another woman, but I could tell she wanted me to come over, say something, look at my son. I ignored her and followed Deidre out of the restaurant. What kind of man does that make me?"

Jace walked in front of him and stopped, looking down. "Doesn't matter what happened back then. What matters now is how you handle it with Kade going forward."

"You saw the look on his face, heard his voice. He hates me."

"No. He hates what you did. Kade doesn't know you as a person and now's your opportunity." Jace clasped his brother on the shoulder. "He's staying in a cabin a few miles away. Of course, you'll stay here tonight."

"I have a room in town."

"Stay here, Rafe. Let the room go," Heath said and stood, stretching his hands above his head. "I'll show you where he's staying. From there, it's up to you."

******

Kade didn't know where he planned to ride. He only knew he had to get away from there and ride fast and

233

hard—just him and the bike. He pulled onto the highway and turned away from town.

He'd seen the look of surprise and disbelief on Brooke's face, the same as everyone else except Heath and Jace. They'd known who he was before he announced it during his outburst. God, what had he been thinking? He should've confronted Rafe in private, or not at all.

The miles passed under a clear sky that had turned jet black with a million bright stars providing the only light. Beautiful didn't describe it, yet he didn't allow himself to enjoy it.

Kade continued to berate himself for not keeping his mouth shut and his temper under control. What did he expect Rafe to do? Admit in front of everyone he had a bastard son he'd never acknowledged? He'd interrogated enough people to be able to read small changes in their eyes, their expressions. Rafe knew, maybe had always known, yet he'd let Kade and his mother struggle alone.

He turned onto a side road Eric had once taken him on. It led into a national forest. You could travel for miles without seeing another car. He'd ride a few more miles, turn around, and head for his cabin. Seeing Brooke tonight wouldn't happen, not in his current mood. Besides, what could be said she didn't already know? The best decision would be to pack up and head to San Diego, forget the rest of his leave, the ranch, and Brooke. She deserved better.

Four miles up the road he came to a fork and made the decision to turn back. Kade made a U-turn at the same time he heard the rumble of motorcycle engines in the distance. He stopped and waited, seeing no lights as the noise became louder. Shit. Not only had he set himself up, he'd ridden off without any identification or protection. His gun was under the seat of his truck, his ankle knife on his dresser at the cabin. He revved his motor, let out the clutch and started forward. Playing chicken wasn't a great option, but it was a helluva lot better than anything else he could come up with.

Kade accelerated, seeing the outline of four riders ahead, two in front, two behind, taking up both lanes. He couldn't make out their bikes or identifying marks, but his instincts told him Satan's Brethren had found him.

He took the middle of the road. If he couldn't get past them, and if they moved to the inside, he might be able to take a couple down with him. It might be suicide, but so was doing nothing.

Fifty yards, forty, thirty. He lowered his head, focused on going straight through the middle. They began to move toward the center. Perfect. He'd done this before and come through with minor injuries. Ten yards. He jagged one way then the other, kicking out and causing the first two to falter enough to go off the road. He began to slide as the other two came at him. Kade turned his wheel hard to the left, causing his bike to go down. He low-sided, skidding into the path of the next two, registering lights coming up from the distance a moment before his body hit the pavement. Pain sliced through him and he could feel a crushing sensation in his chest just before everything went black.

******

Heath woke to the sound of pounding on the front door. He looked at the clock—two in the morning. No news at this hour could be good. He grabbed a robe and dashed downstairs, pulling the door open to see DEA Agent Clive Nelson and Police Chief Towers.

"Buck, Agent Nelson. Come in."

They walked a few feet into the house, then stopped and looked up as Trey and Rafe came down the stairs.

"There's been an accident. Kade's in intensive care."

"What? When?" Rafe stepped forward, worry etched on his face.

"A few hours ago. It's a long story and I'll be glad to explain it all, but we thought you'd want to know right away."

"I'll grab a coat and be right down." Rafe dashed up the stairs, as did Trey and Heath. Five minutes later they were ready to leave.

"We'll take two cars. Rafe, why don't you ride with me?" Heath shut the door, sending an encouraging look at Annie and Jesse, who stood at the base of the stairs.

They followed Chief Towers' car to the hospital and dashed straight to intensive care.

Chapter Seventeen

"May I help you?"

Rafe stepped up. "My son, Kade Taylor MacLaren. I understand he's here."

The nurse looked at the intake log then back up at Rafe. "Let me get his doctor for you. Please, have a seat."

They joined Buck and Clive in the waiting room.

"What happened?" Heath asked.

"Agent Nelson knows more about it than I do," Buck said.

"I can't give you all the details, but—"

"Where is he? Can I see him?" Brooke burst into the room, her hands shaking, her breath unsteady as she dashed to Heath. He stood and wrapped his arms around her.

"We're waiting for his doctor." He looked at Rafe, who stood with his arms crossed, staring into the distance. "Rafe, this is Kade's good friend, and my stepdaughter, Brooke, and her friend, Paige."

Brooke walked over to him and put a hand on his arm. "Kade's a very special man. I'm sure you'll realize it once you get a chance to know him." Her voice wavered, then cracked as she buried her face in her hands. Paige placed an arm around her friend and led her to a nearby chair.

Rafe said nothing as he worked to control the emotions rolling through him. The son he'd never reached out to, never acknowledged, lay in critical condition a hundred feet away and he might never get a chance to know him. Reyna was the most beautiful, kind, and giving woman he'd ever known, and he loved her beyond reason. When she disappeared he went crazy, doing everything he could to find her, but failed. When he'd seen her a few years later, with Kade, he'd been so stunned and angry, he'd walked away, knowing in his heart he was making a huge mistake. Now, God willing, he might have a chance to atone for some of the damage he'd caused.

"...Satan's Brethren." Rafe heard Clive mention the name of an outlaw motorcycle gang he'd read about in the papers. Mean group into all kinds of illegal activities.

"What about Satan's Brethren?" Rafe asked.

"Kade is scheduled to testify against several of the gang leaders when they go to trial. We thought he'd be fine here, in Fire Mountain, but they found him. That's who he tangled with tonight." Clive glanced at Brooke to see her eyes widen at his words.

"How'd you find him?" Brooke asked.

"We've been tracking the group. When several of them found their way here, my captain sent me and two others to keep a twenty-four hour watch on them and Kade. I followed him when he left the ranch tonight. My partners were parked a couple hundred yards away at a local bar where the Brethren were hanging out. They saw

Kade pass by, jumped on their bikes, and followed him. My team and I were right behind them."

"Thank God," Brooke breathed out.

Clive stood and paced to the window, then turned back. "I know he's in bad shape, but that man's been through worse—much worse. He's strong with one of the keenest survival instincts of anyone I've ever met."

The door swung open as the doctor walked in and looked around.

"I'm Doctor Beckwith."

"I'm Rafe MacLaren, Kade's father. How is he?"

Beckwith looked around at the others, nodding at Heath, whom he recognized.

"It's all right to talk in front of them. They're family." Rafe shot a look to Heath and Trey, then back to the doctor.

"He's an incredibly lucky man. A couple of broken ribs, some torn ligaments, various lacerations. The worst is the concussion. We found no internal injuries, which is a miracle given the way he went down. He's in intensive care and will remain there overnight and more than likely through tomorrow."

"Can I see him?" Rafe asked.

"Two at most tonight, one at a time and just for a few minutes each."

Rafe followed him to Kade's room to see bandages covering a good portion of his son's body. He had to remind himself none of the injuries were life-threatening even though he looked like he'd been rolled in a cement mixer.

He stood next to the bed, a part of him glad Kade couldn't see the fear that had gripped him from the moment he'd heard his son had been in accident. His oldest son, the one he had yet to get to know. Rafe glanced at the monitors and tubes, wishing there were something more he could do. He stood frozen a couple more minutes then lifted a hand and clasped Kade's arm in a gentle squeeze, closing his eyes tight. He took a shaky breath, let go of Kade's arm, and walked from the room.

"How is he?" Brooke asked when Rafe joined them in the waiting room.

"He didn't stir, which is probably good. Do you want to go in?" he asked her.

"Yes, please."

Rafe walked with her down the hall and pointed to Kade's bed. "I'll be waiting with the others." He left her staring through the glass window.

Kade had always seemed so indestructible with his tall, strong physique, his 'don't mess with me' attitude, and enviable self-confidence. She admired the way he approached life—straight on with no comprehension of failure. The only time she'd seen him vulnerable was tonight, when he'd confronted his father. Her heart still slammed in her chest at the impact his announcement made.

Brooke wiped damp hands down her jeans before walking toward the bed. He didn't stir as she pulled a chair next to the bed and lowered herself into the seat. The monitors beeped a steady rhythm, indicating his vital signs were holding up even though the bruising and bandages signaled injuries requiring time and patience to heal.

She reached out and laid a hand on his, a quiet prayer escaping her lips. There remained so much to be said and she found herself hoping he'd give them a chance to work through the obstacles he believed would keep them apart. Brooke knew better. She'd already made up her mind about Kade and what she wanted—nothing less than his love and a lifetime together.

She squeezed his hand and began to release it when he tightened the grip. Her eyes snapped to his, which were mere slits.

"Hey." She leaned closer, an uncertain smile curving her lips.

"Hey." His strained, raspy voice triggered a sense of relief and she let out a breath in a slow stream.

"If you didn't want to see me again, all you had to do was tell me. You didn't have to go to this extreme. You look like hell." She chuckled, more from relief than humor.

He squeezed her hand once more. "You look beautiful," he managed before his eyes flickered shut and he drifted back to sleep.

She held his hand another minute, then left the room, looking at his prone form once more before returning to waiting room. All eyes turned to her when she entered the waiting room.

"He woke for a few seconds, and he recognized me." Relief washed over her as she collapsed into the embrace Heath offered.

"Well, I'd better take off," Clive said as he stood. "I'll be back in a few hours." He walked out the door leaving Brooke, Paige, Rafe, Heath, and Trey alone. Chief Towers had gone back to the station while Rafe was with Kade, saying he'd check back late morning.

"I need coffee," Trey said and pushed from his chair.

"We all could use a break." Heath glanced at his watch. "The cafeteria should be open by now." He looked at Brooke who hadn't budged. "Come on, honey. They have my cell number and I'll let them know where we're headed."

Brooke didn't want to leave, although she doubted they'd let her or Rafe back in Kade's room for a while. She nodded and followed the others to the elevator, glancing over her shoulder toward Kade's room once more as they disappeared into a hallway.

******

The hours passed as they waited for another chance to see Kade. Trey had been reluctant to leave, but he and Jesse had a plane to catch for their return to the base. Heath told him they'd be in touch as soon as they knew anything further.

242

Jace and Caroline stopped by for a while before Eric, Cam, and Cassie joined them, leaving Annie at home to watch Trevor.

"Is there a Brooke here?" A nurse poked her head into the room and glanced around.

"I'm Brooke."

"Mr. Taylor is awake and asking for you."

She looked at the others then followed the nurse down the hall.

"Actually, he didn't so much ask, he more demanded we find you," the nurse said, amusement lacing her voice. "I have to warn you, he insists on leaving. Of course that won't happen. He's not going anywhere until the doctor releases him."

Brooke walked in to see Kade trying to sit up.

"What in the world are you doing?" Brooke asked as she approached the bed and glared down at him.

"The doctor says all I've got are a few broken ribs and a concussion—"

"And torn ligaments."

He scowled at her. "I've had worse and I want out of here."

"Don't even think about it. If you do, I'll get Eric, Cam, Heath, and your father, who are all right down the hall. Trust me, you do not want to go there."

The mention of his father stalled him, but only for a moment. "You forget, I'm not part of your extended tribe. I don't need their blessing to leave."

"You most certainly are a part of the family. You're a MacLaren for crying out loud, which means, you're more a member than I am." Her firm voice held hints of both reprimand and exasperation as she checked to be sure he hadn't dislodged any tubes. "Has anyone ever told you how infuriating you can be?"

Kade stared at her, his lips pursed into a thin line which began to tip up at the corners the angrier she became. He'd never seen her quite this irate—face reddening, nostrils flaring, and eyes shooting sparks his way. He liked this side of her, even if it was directed at him.

"A couple of people have mentioned it, yes." His eyes crinkled in amusement.

"Are you laughing at me?" Her hands were fisted on her hips, daring him to deny it.

"Never."

Brooke recognized the lie the moment it left his lips. She began to relax, the stress on her face easing. "Good," she said as she pulled up a chair. "You look much better than you did twelve hours ago."

"I feel better, especially since I refused to take any more of the pain killers they've been pouring down me. My head feels like it's splitting open, but I can deal with it. I've—"

"I know. You've been through much worse," she snorted and crossed her arms across her chest. "Guess what, Galahad, you aren't in charge here."

Kade caught her stare and felt a welcome calm wash over him. He'd never felt this sense of comfort, rightness with any woman other than Brooke. He wanted to hold onto it forever.

"I'm beginning to realize that." He tried again to lift his head and grimaced as pain sliced behind his eyes. "How's my bike?"

"Eric says it may be salvageable. He trailered it to the house so you could make a decision when you get home."

"You mentioned Rafe."

"Your father," she corrected in a soft voice.

"Yeah, whatever. Is he still here?"

"He refused to leave. We thought they'd kick us all out as much as he badgered the nurses about your condition. You know, he's been in here several times to check on you. He'd have stayed the entire time, but they wouldn't let him."

"I don't remember him being in here." He closed his eyes, sorry he'd even mentioned his father.

"You need to give him a chance, Kade. Maybe there's a story you don't know."

He opened his eyes, letting them scan the room before focusing on Brooke. "Maybe." His eyes flickered and Brooke knew he needed rest.

"I'd better go."

"Not yet. Stay. I need to tell you something." His voice began to slur as exhaustion overtook him.

"Can't it wait until you've rested?" she asked.

"I love you, Brooke." The words came out as his head bobbed and his eyes closed.

Her heart slammed in her chest, his announcement taking her by surprise. She prayed someday she'd hear it, yet hadn't expected it would be today. She watched for a moment, confirming he'd fallen asleep, then leaned over and placed a kiss on his cheek. "I love you too, Kade."

******

"Are you certain you can't keep him a couple more days?" Brooke quipped as Kade argued with a nurse about being rolled out in a wheelchair.

"Not on your life. This man is ready to go, and go he will. In *this* chair."

"I can use crutches."

"Yes, you can, Mr. Taylor. When you get home and not before. Now, let me help you into this chair." She rolled it to the side of the bed where Kade sat, dressed, and ready to bolt. As soon as she pulled it to a stop, he eased off the bed and dropped into the seat, a self-satisfied grin on his face.

"Such a child," Brooke murmured, shaking her head.

She walked next to the chair as the nurse wheeled him outside to the waiting SUV. Heath, Jace, and Rafe stood next to it, smiles on two faces, a pensive expression on the third.

Rafe stepped forward. "How can I help?" he asked the nurse, ignoring the distrustful look in Kade's eyes.

Kade didn't protest when Rafe did as the nurse said and assisted him into the back seat.

"You okay?" Rafe asked.

Kade nodded and leaned his head against the seat.

Brooke climbed into the middle with Rafe on the other side. She felt like a buffer between the two. She had to hand it to Rafe, he'd left the hospital just threes time over the last few days to clean up, returning within a couple of hours to take his usual seat in the waiting room.

She felt Kade's hand on hers and looked over to see a weary smile cross his face. He pulled their joined hands toward him to rest in his lap, then closed his eyes again. The broken ribs and torn ligaments in his knee would take time to heal, the latter requiring the services of an orthopedist as well as physical therapy. Between Eric's motorcycle accident a few years before and Annie being hit by a drunk driver, the family had a solid list of professionals for Kade to see.

A question hung in Brooke's mind. Would he choose to recuperate in Fire Mountain or return to San Diego and into the fold of the DEA?

Heath pulled to a stop in front of the ranch house, killed the engine, and turned toward the back seat.

"You'll be staying with us a few nights, Kade. Any arguments and we'll put Trevor in your room to keep you company."

Annie stood at the front door, relief flashing across her face at the sight of Kade exiting the car, Jace on one side and Rafe on the other. Heath and Brooke followed

247

behind, carrying a set of crutches and a collapsible wheelchair.

"It's great to see you," Annie said and pushed the door wide.

"A little different than the way I left the other night."

"It is. You're not angry." Annie met his gaze, hoping he understood her meaning.

He looked up at her and nodded. "You got me there."

"You'll be in the bedroom behind the family room. It's where I stayed after my accident." Annie led the way, even though everyone knew which room she meant. "Here you go."

Jace and Rafe helped Kade onto the bed, lifting his injured knee up as Brooke slid a pillow under it. Rafe stayed close to the edge of the bed as if trying to decide if he should leave or say what had been on his mind for days. Jace glanced at the others, jerking his head toward the door in an effort to give the father and son some privacy. They took the cue, Brooke taking up the rear.

"Where are you going?" Kade asked, his eyes darting toward her, a decidedly uncomfortable look on his face.

Rafe looked over his shoulder at Brooke, grateful for the time alone with Kade.

"I'll be right back. Promise." She shut the door, not giving him time to protest.

Chapter Eighteen

Kade shifted on the bed, trying to ease the aching in his ribs. Every time he breathed, coughed, sneezed, or laughed, pain shot through him. He'd suffered the same injury before and knew it would take time to heal. The discomfort would continue until the bones mended, and even then, they'd be sore for months. Kade looked up at the sound of Rafe clearing his throat.

His father shifted from one foot to the other, shoving his hands in his pockets as his eyes locked on Kade's.

"This probably isn't the best time to talk. I just want you to know I'm here, when you're ready." Rafe turned and walked to the door, reaching for the handle.

"Why?"

Rafe knew what Kade asked, he just didn't know how to answer him. He slowly turned toward the bed, noting his son's emotionless expression. The green eyes, so much like his own, were all that gave away how much Rafe's answer meant to him.

"Reyna never told me about you."

"The other night...I could see it in your eyes. You knew."

Rafe stepped closer to the bed. "I suspected." He let out a shallow breath. No excuse would make up for the lost years. "I hadn't seen your mother since she left me, before you were born. When our paths crossed years later, she sat in a booth in a small diner where we used to meet. She had a little boy next to her. The same hair, same eyes as mine."

"Me."

"Yes. Now I know it was you. At the time, however, she never let on, didn't say a word or try to get in touch with me. I let it go." He lowered himself onto the bed and ran a hand through his hair. "Weeks later, I tried to find her. After another few weeks without success, I gave up, figuring she'd disappeared as she had years before."

"She went by Taylor back then. Reyna Santiago Taylor." Kade's flat voice tore at Rafe's heart. "She made up the last name, telling people my father had died so they wouldn't think less of me."

"Your birth certificate shows MacLaren."

"She wanted me to have my rightful heritage, even if you never acknowledged me."

"Shit," Rafe mumbled, stood and paced to the window in frustration. "Why didn't she just tell me, come to me?"

Kade stared at his father, then looked down at his injured knee, wishing he could get up and pace, or throw something. Anything other than sit there in forced calm wishing he had the answer to that question. "I don't know." He leaned against the headboard and closed his eyes, remembering the day he'd found his birth certificate.

He and his mother had returned from a dinner celebrating his thirteenth birthday. His mother asked him

250

to go into her room and look under the bed. He got on his hands and knees, pulled up the bedspread, and found a wrapped present next to a box he'd never seen before. Curious, he'd pulled it out and opened it to find an envelope with his name scrawled across the top—Kade Santiago Taylor MacLaren. Inside he found his birth certificate.

He'd always gone by Kade Taylor, the last name his mother used, never suspecting another name existed. When he'd asked her about it, she'd broken down, told him about Rafe, and begged him not to approach him. He honored his mother's wishes.

"Is she still in Crooked Tree?"

"She lives in Mexico with her mother's relatives. Once in a while she comes for a visit, but not often. I usually fly down to see her."

Rafe walked the few steps to the bed. "You're my son, Kade. I don't know what I can say or do to make things right, but I can promise you I'll do whatever is needed to gain your trust."

Kade thought he was too old to feel the kind of choking emotion those words caused. His throat closed, making speech impossible.

Rafe laid a hand on his son's shoulder. "We'll talk later." He walked from the room, closing the door behind him.

******

Brooke knocked on the door to Kade's room, holding a plate loaded with eggs and bacon. She'd checked on him three times after Rafe had left his room the day before. He'd either been asleep or had chosen to fake it each time. Brooke believed he needed time to come to terms with whatever Rafe had told him and left him alone. By nine that evening, she'd given up and gone to bed.

Everyone had left Rafe to himself after his time with Kade. He didn't volunteer what had been said and no one dared pry, believing the attempt he'd made to be alone with his son said a lot about his intentions.

Brooke tapped once more before peering into the room. He lay on his back, one arm stretched above his head, eyes closed. He appeared to be asleep. She set the plate down and opened the blinds, letting the morning sun wash over the bed and onto his face. Still nothing. He'd been awake most of his last two days in the hospital, grumbling about going home and being a general pain in the ass. Something didn't make sense.

Brooke sat on the edge of the bed and stroked a finger down his face, feeling his two-day stubble. Her thumb rubbed across his lower lip, then traced a line along the upper one. When he didn't budge, she became bolder, letting her finger run a path down his neck. The sheet had been pushed to his hips, exposing the crisp hair across his chest that narrowed as it descended toward his waist and hips, then disappeared below the sheet.

She glanced up, noting he still lay quiet, breathing in a soft rhythm. Brooke's courage rose as she splayed her hand across his chest, feeling the silky hairs and taut muscles underneath. She swallowed a small lump in her throat and let her hand move lower to his stomach, to the edge of the sheet. She paused briefly before sliding her fingers below the cotton cover. She was inches from her goal when a hand thrust out and grasped her wrist. She shrieked as her eyes darted to Kade.

"Something you want?"

She couldn't mistake the warning in his thick, raspy voice. She bit her lower lip and tried to pull her hand free. He tightened his grip.

"Well?"

She straightened her spine and jutted her chin out. "Yes. As a matter of fact, there is something I want."

"And what is that?"

"I want you to stop pretending you're asleep when I come into the room. It's becoming quite annoying."

One side of Kade's mouth lifted as he drew her toward him, wrapping his free arm around her waist, and pulling her close. "Annoying, huh?"

Her breath hitched as her gaze moved to his mouth and the full lips which were slightly parted. She glanced at his eyes and her heart tripped over itself at the smoldering, bold stare. Her tongue darted out to moisten her lips. Before she could register his intent, he'd drawn her down, his mouth covering hers in a kiss both hungry and searching.

He lessened the pressure. His lips felt warm as they brushed across hers, gentle and persuasive. He held her tight, not wanting to let go, ever. Kade raised his mouth from hers, letting his gaze move from her lips, swollen from his kisses, to her glazed eyes.

His arms moved from around her and he grasped both her hands in his, kissing her fingers before holding them to his chest.

Brooke leaned toward him, her heart pounding as she waited.

"My captain called last night. I need to return to San Diego to testify in at least one trial. I could be gone a few days or weeks—there's no way of knowing right now."

There was more—she was certain of it.

"What are you trying to tell me?" Fear gripped her. He sounded as if he might be saying goodbye instead of what she'd been hoping for since he'd told her he loved her.

He couldn't remember any time in his life he'd felt more nervous. Something about his feelings for Brooke messed with his mind as well as his self-confidence. She broke down his defenses, opening up vulnerabilities he thought were long ago buried.

"Did you know Heath, Jace, and Rafe came in to talk with me late last night?"

The surprised look on her face told him she didn't.

"It appears the three of them have worked out their differences enough for the deal to go through to buy RTC and Rafe will stay on as president. It's hard to explain as I don't fully understand it yet, but the short version is, they've offered me a job. I'd be helping in various capacities in two areas—stock for pleasure riding and lessons, and bucking stock operations, both broncs and bulls." He said, and shook his head. He could feel the tension pouring from Brooke, knowing she wondered where all this was heading.

"And?" She edged closer to him on the bed.

"I said yes."

She launched herself into his arms, wrapping hers around his neck, trying not to put pressure on his broken ribs.

"Under one condition," Kade added in a somber tone against her ear.

Brooke pulled back and held her breath.

"I'd only stay if you agreed to marry me."

She clasped a hand over her mouth, not quite believing what she'd heard. Her eyes shone as she shook her head in two slow movements—up, then down.

Kade placed a finger under her chin and lifted her face to him. "Does that mean yes?'

She cupped his face with her hands and placed a soft kiss on his lips. "Yes. Absolutely, yes."

Epilogue

Six months later...

They packed for their trip back to Fire Mountain, accepting their honeymoon had come to an end. When Brooke first said she wanted a wedding between Christmas and New Year's, Kade had balked, wanting a quick ceremony to remove any chance she'd change her mind. She'd held firm, saying by then he'd be finished with the rehabilitation on his knee, his ribs would be healed, and most of the family could attend. It all made sense. Still, six months seemed like a long time to a man who wanted her in his life, and in his bed, on a daily basis.

They'd gotten together with Paige and Nesto twice during their time in San Diego. Both traveled to Fire Mountain for the wedding, along with Clive Nelson. Nesto and Clive stood up with Kade, while Paige and Cassie were Brooke's bridesmaids.

"What do you want to do on our last night here?" he asked, wrapping his arms around her, pulling her against his chest and nuzzling her neck. She let out a sigh, tempting him to pick her up and lay her across the king size bed, making the decision for both of them.

"Would it be all right if we ate at the Sea Chalet then took a walk?"

He knew what she wanted. The small, locals hangout had been her favorite place to pick up a quick dinner after her runs on the beach. Sometimes she'd take her meal back toward her spot on the sand, sit on her towel, and take her time working her way through the delicious food. For weeks he'd sat on his bike on the cliff overhead and watched, wanting nothing more than to walk down the dirt path and take a seat alongside. Now he could.

"I can't think of anything I'd rather do."

She quirked a brow at him.

"Well, maybe one other thing," he smiled, turning her toward him, lowering his mouth to hers in a slow, burning kiss.

A few hours later, they picked up their food and threw their towels on a quiet stretch of beach. The sun had just begun to set with low clouds highlighting the stormy colors of blue and gray in the sky. The rays of the setting sun peeked under the clouds, throwing an almost iridescent, orange glow on the sand, which was littered with small rocks and broken shells. Crashing waves provided the background music as they ate their final meal along the shore of San Diego. Both knew they'd return, but never again as newlyweds.

"What do Heath and Jace have you working on when we return?" Kade asked, enjoying the cool breeze. He'd fulfilled his last obligations with the DEA and would be starting work for his family when they returned. Kade and his father still had a ways to go defining their relationship, but he couldn't turn his back on the

MacLarens after every one of them had welcomed him with open arms. He'd even started using his given name, Kade MacLaren.

"I'll travel to the Cold Creek operation to review my assessment with their senior team. Cam set it up just before our wedding. Plus, Heath and Jace have been interviewing candidates for a marketing position. They say they've made their decision and plan to introduce the new person to everyone after I return from Colorado."

"Do you know anything about the person?"

"Not much, other than she's someone they met at the Cattleman's Convention last fall. Apparently she has quite a portfolio in a new venture they'd like to pursue. She'll also be working closely with Eric in the land development group."

Kade grabbed her hand. "Well, they do have a history of hiring the best." He smiled at her and placed a kiss on her palm. He fell back onto the towel, pulling her on top of him, both laughing as he threaded his fingers through her hair and caressed her back.

"I've wanted to do this since the first time I laid eyes on you. Sitting on my chopper, watching you on the beach, reading a book. I couldn't take my eyes off you. At the same time, I never allowed myself to think I'd ever get a chance to be here beside you. I'd spent so many nights working or alone that I didn't realize how much I wanted to spend them with someone special. I didn't know how lonely my nights had become until I met you."

She lifted her head, smiling as he pushed an errant strand of hair from her face and gave her a brief kiss. "Do you know what I cherish the most?" she asked, snuggling against his chest.

"No. What?"

"Now I have all your nights."

******

Join me in the continuation of the MacLarens of Fire Mountain Contemporary series with Always Love You, Book Five

A painful past separates them...but their shared passion won't let them forget. Start reading **Always Love You** to find out if a second chance is in their future!

If you want to keep current on all my preorders, new releases, and other happenings, sign up for my newsletter at: https://www.shirleendavies.com/contact-me.html

A Note from Shirleen

Thank you for taking the time to read **All Your Nights**!

If you enjoyed it, please consider telling your friends or posting a short review. Word of mouth is an author's best friend and much appreciated.

I care about quality, so if you find something in error, please contact me via email at shirleen@shirleendavies.com.

Books by Shirleen Davies

Contemporary Western Romance Series

MacLarens of Fire Mountain

Second Summer, Book One
Hard Landing, Book Two
One More Day, Book Three
All Your Nights, Book Four
Always Love You, Book Five
Hearts Don't Lie, Book Six
No Getting Over You, Book Seven
'Til the Sun Comes Up, Book Eight
Foolish Heart, Book Nine

Macklins of Whiskey Bend

Thorn, Book One
Del, Book Two
Boone, Book Three

Historical Western Romance Series
Redemption Mountain

Redemption's Edge, Book One
Wildfire Creek, Book Two

Sunrise Ridge, Book Three
Dixie Moon, Book Four
Survivor Pass, Book Five
Promise Trail, Book Six
Deep River, Book Seven
Courage Canyon, Book Eight
Forsaken Falls, Book Nine
Solitude Gorge, Book Ten
Rogue Rapids, Book Eleven
Angel Peak, Book Twelve
Restless Wind, Book Thirteen
Storm Summit, Book Fourteen
Mystery Mesa, Book Fifteen
Thunder Valley, Book Sixteen
A Very Splendor Christmas, Holiday Novella, Book Seventeen
Paradise Point, Book Eighteen,
Silent Sunset, Book Nineteen
Rocky Basin, Book Twenty, Coming Next in the Series!

MacLarens of Fire Mountain

Tougher than the Rest, Book One
Faster than the Rest, Book Two
Harder than the Rest, Book Three
Stronger than the Rest, Book Four
Deadlier than the Rest, Book Five
Wilder than the Rest, Book Six

MacLarens of Boundary Mountain

Colin's Quest, Book One,
Brodie's Gamble, Book Two
Quinn's Honor, Book Three
Sam's Legacy, Book Four
Heather's Choice, Book Five
Nate's Destiny, Book Six
Blaine's Wager, Book Seven
Fletcher's Pride, Book Eight
Bay's Desire, Book Nine
Cam's Hope, Book Ten

Romantic Suspense

Eternal Brethren, Military Romantic Suspense

Steadfast, Book One
Shattered, Book Two
Haunted, Book Three
Untamed, Book Four
Devoted, Book Five
Faithful, Book Six
Exposed, Book Seven
Undaunted, Book Eight
Resolute, Book Nine
Unspoken, Book Ten
Defiant, Book Eleven, Coming Next in the Series!

Peregrine Bay, Romantic Suspense

Reclaiming Love, Book One
Our Kind of Love, Book Two
Edge of Love, Book Three, Coming Next in the Series!
Find all of my books at:
https://www.shirleendavies.com/books.html

About Shirleen

Shirleen Davies writes romance—historical, contemporary, and romantic suspense. She grew up in Southern California, attended Oregon State University, and has degrees from San Diego State University and the University of Maryland. Her passion is writing emotionally charged stories of flawed people who find redemption through love and acceptance. She now lives with her husband in a beautiful town in northern Arizona.

I love to hear from my readers!

Send me an email: shirleen@shirleendavies.com
Visit my Website: https://www.shirleendavies.com/
Sign up to be notified of New Releases: https://www.shirleendavies.com/contact/
Follow me on Amazon: http://www.amazon.com/author/shirleendavies
Follow me on BookBub: https://www.bookbub.com/authors/shirleen-davies

Other ways to connect with me:

Facebook Author Page: http://www.facebook.com/shirleendaviesauthor
Twitter: www.twitter.com/shirleendavies
Pinterest: http://pinterest.com/shirleendavies
Instagram: https://www.instagram.com/shirleendavies_author/

Made in the USA
Monee, IL
18 December 2023

49686146R00154